Amish Obsessed

Sarah Amberson

Published by Trellis Publishing, 2021.

AMISH OBSESSED

First edition. July 1, 2021.

ISBN: 979-8224533633

Written by Sarah Amberson.

AMISH OBSESSED

SARAH AMBERSON

David slammed his empty glass unto the counter. He wasn't sure how many he had drunk already, but he wasn't planning on stopping anytime soon.

"David, I think you've had enough. Don't you agree?" Frank, the bartender asked, leaning against the counter.

"Frank, just pour me another. Since when do you care how much I drink?"

"I care since I'm your friend."

"Just because we're friends doesn't mean that you have a say in how much I drink," David growled.

"What are you so upset about this time?" Frank pulled up a high stool and poured David another drink and one for himself.

"Alice. She left me."

Frank began to laugh, and David gave him a glare.

"Why in heaven's name would you care? You never keep a girl around for longer than a week or two anyway."

"I don't care. I mean it was bound to happen, but *she* left *me*. There's a difference, you know."

Frank shrugged his shoulders and rolled his eyes as if he truly couldn't see the difference.

"You know, it's not just that either. My father has been on me about coming back to the company again."

"Now that, is something worthy of a drink. But you my friend have had more than four. That's definitely enough for one night." Frank took the bottle and put it back in its place, ignoring David's groan of protest. "In my opinion you should tell your father exactly where you stand, get yourself a proper girl and get on with your life." Frank shook his head.

"Good advice Frank, good advice. Except my father pays my bills and there ain't a proper girl I care to meet. You know, since you won't be helping me out anymore, I think I should go for a walk."

When Frank nodded in agreement it only made David angrier. Some sort of friend Frank was. Of course, he couldn't expect him to understand his situation.

David pulled out a small worn map of the area from his pocket. Whenever he got a chance to go hiking, he picked a new location. Walking did something for him.

It helped him forget his problems, it helped him get away from his over controlling father and the women who he kept being pushed to be with.

There was something about the peacefulness of being in the forest and away from the city that calmed him. Of course, if anyone ever asked him, David would deny it.

Hiking wasn't exactly an activity that made you look cool and tough which was who David was of course.

There was a little section of woods that David had been waiting to explore for the past two weeks. It was near an Amish community way out in the sticks.

While David had no interest in the Amish community, that section of woods looked particularly interesting for an explore.

Still with an angry scowl on his face he set off.

It took a while for his anger from earlier to wear off, but eventually, he began to enjoy his surroundings. He had walked nearly and hour and a half and the farms seemed to get further apart as he went.

The road gave way to gravel and he found an area that appeared to be a path and began to follow it into the woods. The trees were swaying in a light breeze and the birds where singing cheerfully.

The day was pleasantly warm, and he began to feel more at peace with himself as he walked. David kicked a rock out of his path, as he did so, the tip of his shoe caught on a hidden tree root.

Before he could catch himself, he flew off the path. He expected to land uncomfortably on the side of the path, but instead, he continued to roll down the embankment.

When he finally came to a stop, he felt bruises and bumps all over his body. He pulled himself up against a nearby tree with a groan.

I've got to remember to be more careful in the future.

David reached underneath him to grab something that was poking into his lower back. He was surprised when he felt the corner of a metal box.

Scooting backwards he turned and brushed the leaves off of the box.

It looked old fashioned and like it had been used a lot. It had little spots of rust on the corner and made a creaking sound when he opened it.

Inside there was what looked like a stack of letters and a folded piece of paper that was thicker than the other paper in the box.

Curiosity overcoming him, David unfolded the piece of paper first. It was a portrait of a young man.

It looked as if it had been done with a charcoal pencil and it was so accurate a person could almost mistake it for a photo.

The young man had large eyes that looked intelligent and curious. His curly hair fell over his forehead and he had a dimpled smile as if he was amused with the person drawing the picture.

There was something captivating about the picture, and David took several minutes to study it before he folded it up and put it back.

He then pulled out the letters. They were addressed and had dates on them, but it appeared as if they weren't received letters. It looked as if someone had intended to send them but had never gotten around to it.

David felt a pang of guilt as he flipped through the letters looking for the first one. He probably shouldn't be reading these, but who knew if the owner was still around anyway?

David fought a smirk as he realized that wasn't a good argument. Some of the dates were recent. The newest one was only a week old.

He pulled out the oldest one. It was from eight months ago. He opened the unsealed envelope and pulled out the letter.

The writing was neat and easy to read in black ink.

Dear Mary,

I know I shouldn't' be writing to you. I don't even know where to send the letters since you haven't lived at your old address for two years now.

I just can't do this anymore. Ever since you left, I have no one to talk to. I know you would understand if you were here.

We buried Mark today. I cried when they put the coffin in the ground. I promised I wouldn't, but I couldn't help it.

Nobody knows, but it was my fault he died. I thought you should know that. If you were here, you would try to talk me out of that and tell me it wasn't my fault but I know that it is.

Someone is coming, I have to go. I shouldn't save this. I shouldn't have even written this down, but I feel better now.

Till next time,

Hannah

David flipped the page over and searched the envelope making sure that there wasn't any more written on it.

How had Mark died and why did Hanna think that it was her fault?

David's conscience prickled once more as he opened the next letter. It was dated two months later than the first one.

Dear Mary

I wasn't planning on writing again, but then, maybe you'll send me your real address one day and I'll change the address on my letters and send them to you, who knows?

I wish you were here. You would know what to do. Uncle wants me to marry and he's already arranged it. I agreed only because I didn't have much choice.

I know my uncle doesn't want me around anymore. I remind him too much of what happened with Mark.

The thing is, if I just had to marry someone I didn't love, that would be okay, but he wants me to marry Henry.

I can't marry Henry, I just can't. We all know how he is, and I know he hasn't changed. I have to think of something.

I have to go.

Till next time,

Hannah

David reached for the next letter and paused. He thought he heard a rustle in the woods.

He glanced at the black box. If he left these here, he may never get the chance to read them or find out what happened. But he couldn't take the box. Whoever wrote these had written one only a week ago.

The sound was getting close and David knew he needed to get out of there.

He hastily covered the box up with leaves the way he'd found it and took off at a jog.

By the time he made it back to town, he was so baffled by his find in the woods, he could hardly think of anything else.

He looked at his watch and his heart fell. How had it gotten so late? He was supposed to meet his father for dinner in fifteen minutes.

—-*—-

David had to search for the spot where he had rolled off the trail. He backtracked several times before he found the root and the broken branches where he had rolled through the underbrush. He carefully made his way down the steep embankment to the spot where the box had been.

David felt almost afraid of looking under the tree. He expected the box to be gone. Surely whoever had hidden it there had realized it had been touched. Had he put the letters back the way he found them? What about the portrait? Had he folded it right?

David pushed back the leaves and sighed in relief when he spotted the box. It was still there.

It looked the same as last time, though this time when he opened it, he was surprised to find a fresh new letter sitting on top.

Not wanting to read out of order, David shifted through the letters until he found the third one in order according to the dates carefully written in the corner of each one.

Dear Mary

I talked to Henry today. I begged him to refuse to marry me. He laughed. He hasn't changed a bit.

I'm scared and I don't know what to do.

Hannah

A chill ran down David's spine as he re-read the short letter. He felt pity for the girl.

He hurriedly pulled out the next letter. It was dated two months ago. David wondered why Hannah had taken so long to write again.

This one didn't have a physical address on it. It simply had a name scrawled across the front, a name David had seen before.

Dear Mark,

Why am I writing you? You're dead. But I need to write this. Maybe you can read over my shoulder from heaven.

My aunt and uncle are excited about the wedding. I tried to tell them about Henry. That's right, they are making me marry Henry.

No one says it out loud, but we all know how that works. I have tried talking to Henry, but he's looking forward to it too.

We have all heard the stories about him and his last fiancé. Who knows what happened? I suppose I will soon enough.

I want you to know that I will always love you. Even if I give myself to Henry, my heart will always be yours.

Please forgive me for what happened, for losing your life. If I could go back, I would do so much differently.

Your love, forever,

Hannah.

David fought the guilt that started to fill him. Here he was reading some person's private letters. Some things didn't make sense to him. The way Hannah talked about things didn't make sense sometimes.

Eager to find out more, he opened another letter. It was dated back a month and a half.

Dear Mary,

I'm thinking about leaving the community, but I don't know where to go. I wish I would have listened to you when you offered to take me with you when you left.

I don't know anyone out there. At least here, I know what to expect. I've been Amish my whole life. Can I really just leave that behind?

Everyone is planning my wedding. I think they can tell that I'm not excited, but no one seems to care. It's in three months now. I want out. I need out.

Where are you, Mary?

Hannah

She was Amish. Suddenly the pieces fit into place. David knew that there was an Amish community around here. Hannah had to be from there.

David pulled out the last two letters. One was from a week ago and the other was from yesterday.

He pulled out the one that was a week old.

Dear Mary,

I can't leave. One of the elders must have suspected I wanted to. Henry and I are getting Married in two weeks now.

The elder talked to me and told me that if I left, I would have nowhere to live. He says the

Englishers wouldn't help me and that they would try to take advantage of me.

Maybe that's why you never wrote like you said you would, and I have no idea where to send any of these letters.

I'm to scared to leave. I don't think I could do it on my own.

Hannah

David felt his heart swell with anger at the elder. He was trying to control Hannah. Why was there so much pressure to marry this Henry fellow anyway?

Hannah should be able to do what she wanted. David tried to imagine what Hanna looked like. Maybe she had black hair and a big nose, or maybe she had delicate lips and red hair.

He couldn't put a face to the words he had read over the past couple of days.

He pulled out the last letter with sadness. After this, would there still be letters?

According to the date, there was only six days left until she was supposed to marry Henry.

Hanna's words had reached a place in Henry's heart that he thought no longer existed. He realized with a start that he didn't' want Hanna to marry Henry.

He wanted to her to have freedom. Maybe it was because freedom was something that he himself craved, or maybe it was the words from her letters that filled his mind.

David decided he was going to go to that Amish community, and he was going to find Hannah and give her a way out.

—-*—-

Five days. There were only five days left until Hannah was supposed to marry Henry. David wasn't sure if it was this fact, or the fact he might be about to meet the girl from the letters that made him more nervous.

David had heard plenty about the Amish communities, but he had never set foot inside of one.

Children dressed in little dresses and bonnets ran up and down the pathways. There were horses and buggies and all the men had beards.

David walked up to the first house on the street. It was simply built with white doors and windows.

Even though the houses looked slightly different, they were so similar you could tell that they were all planned out or even built by the same people.

After several minutes, a man opened the door. He looked David up and down skeptically and stroked his beard. He wore a black hat and suspenders, just like David had seen Amish men wear around town.

"Can I help you?" the man asked. His eyes were cold and unfriendly, making David fidget.

He wondered if Hannah would get in trouble for him being here. Thinking quickly, he changed what he was going to say. "I'm looking for a Henry."

The man squinted his eyes a little more and shook his head. "There's several Henry's in this community. You'll have to be more specific."

"Ummm, I'm not sure. I met him in town but forgot to ask his last name."

The Amish man gave him a half smile. "I'll let the Henrys in the community know you stopped by. Whichever one you talked to will find you I'm sure." With that, the door closed before David could say anything else.

David groaned. He'd messed up. He wasn't going to be able to find Hannah this way. But he did know of a place she had visited before and if he was lucky she would come there again.

With a new plan formulating in his mind he turned around and left the way he had come.

He wasn't about to give up. He was just getting started.

—-*—-

David felt his eyelids drooping as he watched the letter tree from a distance.

He wasn't sure when he'd started calling it the letter tree. That had just happened, and he thought of it as such. It was as if the tree had taken on a personality, like it knew a secret.

He kept imagining what Hannah would look like. This was the third day he had been siting here all day. There were only two days left until Hannah was supposed to marry Henry. David was beginning to think about trying at the community again.

Suddenly a scuffling sound made him sit up straighter. A young woman appeared from the trees. She was dressed in a light blue dress and had long dark brown hair.

She was crying and she was carrying a notebook, pen and one of the familiar envelopes that David had found in the box.

She walked over to the letter tree and pulled out the metal box. She unfolded the portrait and stared at it for several moments before she set it down and began to write.

David watched her, beginning to sweat on his forehead and back. He had imagined their meeting so many times and now he was afraid of what It would be like in real life.

He took a deep breath and stepped out from the place he had been hiding.

"Hannah?"

Hannah spun around to face him. "Wh- Who are you and how do you know my name?" She wiped the tears from her face in an almost frantic manner and glared at him.

"I- uh."

"You're not Amish." Hannah took a step back and a little glint of fear filled her eyes.

"No, no I'm not. We don't exactly know each other. I know your name from the letters."

Hannah's face first filled with horror and then anger. "You read my letters? You- You nosy Englisher! Didn't you know they were private?"

David ran a hand through his hair. He had imagined their meeting going better than this.

"I didn't mean to. I fell down the hill and just stumbled onto the box and-"

"Nonsense! You didn't mean to? You can't read a letter without meaning to!"

David found himself smiling. Hannah had a little accent that made it almost comical when she yelled and was angry.

"What are you smiling at? You think this is funny?" Hannah gathered up the metal box into her arms and turned to go. "Stay away from me, Englisher," she snapped as she began to walk away.

Seeing her leaving snapped David out of his trance like state. "Wait, wait, wait. You're getting married in two days."

Hannah spun back around. "Yes, I am. I would ask how you know that but..." Hannah held up the box for emphasis.

"I- In the letters, it said you wanted out. I wanted to tell you that if you still do, I would give you a place to stay and help you get on your feet."

"I'm supposed to trust some strange Englisher man who was reading my private letters and waiting for me in the woods? I'm not completely naïve."

David realized she had a point, but it made him want to convince her all the more.

"You shouldn't have to marry a man that you don't love and especially not one that you are scared of."

For a moment, Hannah looked vulnerable. "Sometimes people don't have a choice."

"People always have a choice." David realized how close he was to her. He could almost imagine he could hear her heart beating a little faster, just like his own.

"I just want you to know that you are not alone." David said softly.

"I don't need your help." Hanna's harsh tone was back, and her mask of indifference had covered her face once again.

"If you change your mind, here's my number and my address." David held out a small slip of paper he had prepared. "I don't know what people have told you about Englishers, as you call them, but we are just regular people."

Hannah quickly snatched the paper from his hands and then stalked off into the woods.

David watched her go with a sinking heart. He wanted to take her home with him today. He wanted to get her far away from the man she feared and from the people forcing her to do something she didn't want to do.

David sighed, if only he had met her sooner. He realized with a start that he actually cared about what happened to Hannah. He didn't remember the last time he had really cared about what happened to someone else.

With a frustrated puff of breath, he turned and walked back to town. He had made some progress but not enough. After today, there was only one full day left before Hannah would be married to Henry, and then it would be too late for anyone to help her.

—-*—-

Hannah's heart was full of turmoil as she headed back to the community. Along her way once she was sure that David wasn't following her, she stopped to burry the box under a different tree. She couldn't take it home and risk her uncle finding it.

She looked down at the paper David had given her. That was how she had known his name. It was scrawled across the paper in elegant handwriting above the phone number and house address.

Hannah had been terrified at first. Who was this strange man who had read some of the most intimate things she had ever written down on paper?

But in their short conversation, she had seen an honesty and kindness that she had only seen in one other man's eyes, Mark's.

For a second, the urge to go back to the letter box and look at Mark's face once more nearly turned her around.

She knew it was against the rules to have Mark's drawing. But it wasn't really a photo of him. She had drawn it.

Telling herself that didn't help the guilt much. Hannah sighed. If only Mark were here, they would be married and living in a little house of their own in the Amish community.

Hannah's problems didn't have to do with the community. They really didn't have anything to do with being Amish either.

The fact was she'd been dealt a hard blow in life that could have happened to anyone in any community, but it had happened to her.

She didn't necessarily blame her uncle. He wanted her married and out of his house. Now Henry... there was certainly some blame to be placed there.

Everyone knew he was violent when he was angry, and no one had done anything about it. The very idea of being tied to him for the rest of her life made Hannah cower.

She had been trying to find a way out for months now. She finally had one. Her thumb and forefinger rubbed back and forth over the paper that David had given her.

The question was, could she trust this David? She didn't know anything about him.

And he knew more about her than any person alive did. He had read the pieces of her heart she had placed on paper after all.

The overwhelming aspect of her situation grabbed hold of her for a moment and she let out a grunt of frustration and kicked at a clump of grass.

By the time she had made it home, she knew what she had to do. She didn't have a choice. She either had to agree to live with a man she knew was bad for the rest of her life, or trust in one that might be good.

It wasn't too hard of a choice to make, she would have to take her chances with David.

The sound of the telephone ringing made David leap from the sofa he was sitting on. He had answered every single phone call snice yesterday when he'd given his number to Hannah. So far, it had been a mix of business men calling for his father and the occasion person looking for his aunt.

"David?" he recognized the soft voice immediately.

"Hannah, I wasn't sure whether to expect your call." David gripped the phone nervously. Now that he was actually talking to her he felt bad about what he was doing.

Did he want to help Hannah because he was being selfless, or was he wanting something in return? He began to realize that he cared for Hannah because he had seen into her thoughts and feelings.

Of course, if she didn't want to pursue any friendship after her escape, he wasn't going to make her, but he could hope she would give him a chance.

"David, I've decided I need your help. I can't marry Henry."

David's mind worked quickly as he finalized the plan he had been thinking about ever since he'd decided to help Hannah.

"Okay, can you get to the letter tree by this evening?"

"The letter tree?" Hannah sounded amused and David could almost imagine her pretty face scrunched up with a smirk.

"Yeah, that's what I call it."

"Yes, I think I can get to the letter tree." Despite her confident words, Hannah's voice sounded uncertain.

"Okay, I'll be waiting for you at dusk."

"I'll be there."

The click on the phone from Hannah hanging up left David feeling a little empty. Dusk that evening sounded way to far away.

While he waited, David called the hotel down the street. At first, he had been tempted to bring Hannah to his house, but he wasn't sure if she would be comfortable with that.

Before he knew it, it was time to go to the woods. He slipped out of the house with his backpack on his shoulders and set out.

He was fairly certain that his father wouldn't be around tonight, but if he was, he probably wouldn't expect to see David. David shrugged. It wasn't as if he and his father were super close so he didn't feel bad about hiding his actions from him.

It took a little longer than he expected to get to the letter tree and by the time he did, it was almost dusk. Unable to calm his beating nervous heart, he took to pacing back and forth nearby.

Every single noise made him peer for the trees, looking for Hanna's slim form and worried face.

As every minute passed, David became more ad more agitated. Where was Hannah? Had she called him while he had been gone to say she wouldn't be coming? Had Henry realized she was leaving him?

The different possibilities overwhelmed David.

Finally, he felt defeated and sat down leaning against a tree, letting himself rest a little. It looked as if Hannah wouldn't be coming and like it was too late, after all, tomorrow, she was marrying Henry.

——-*——-

A noise made David jerk awake. It took him a few seconds to remember where he was. He must have fallen asleep against the tree while he was waiting for Hannah.

"David? David are you here?" David searched his pocket for a flashlight. When he turned it on, Hannah was nearly right in front of him and she let out a little shriek of fear.

David leapt to his feet. "It's okay. It's me, David." he said softly. "Sorry, I think I fell asleep."

"Oh, I- I thought someone was following me. We should go quickly. I'm sorry, I didn't mean to take so long. I think Henry suspected and I couldn't get off alone earlier." As Hannah spoke a mile a minute, she kept looking over her shoulder.

Her little white cap stood out in the dark like a beacon. Suddenly a crack of a twig snapping made both of them jump.

David clicked his flashlight off and took Hannah's hand. "Come on, we should get out of here."

David could make out Hannah's nod from the little bit of moonlight that filtered through the trees.

Another sound in the trees made David sure someone was following them.

He thought of asking Hannah to take her cap off, but it wouldn't make much difference. He could see her dress clearly in the moonlight and he wasn't exactly dressed to blend into the dark either.

"Come on, someone *is* following us."

"I'm sorry," Hannah said shakily, and Henry was fairly certain he heard tears in her voice. "I was afraid he would follow us."

"Who, Henry?"

Hannah squeezed his hand and nodded in response. David made a conscience effort not to let his fear show. He knew these woods well and he was almost positive he could get Hannah away safely, or at least he had to try.

The weaved in and out of the trees. The faster they went, the more sounds behind them they heard. Finally, the lights from town greeted them and David let himself relax a little.

The sounds behind them had stopped, whoever had been following wasn't brave enough to follow them into town. David grinned, someone else's cowardice was a blessing tonight.

Once they were safe in the light with other people in the street around them, David turned to Hannah.

"Do you want to go to my house? I live with my father, but he won't mind if you stay for a while. If not, I've found a hotel nearby where you can stay."

Hannah looked scared and undecided for a moment. "I- can we stay at your house?"

David sighed in relief. He really hadn't wanted her to stay in the hotel. He wasn't' sure if he would be able t protect her the same from there.

"Okay. Come on, it's not too far from here."

—-*—-

David had prepared the guest room just in case Hannah decided to stay at the house with them.

He knew that it was nothing fancy, but Hannah didn't seem disappointed. In fact she seemed to like it.

"Are you okay?" David asked after several moments of awkward silence.

She looked at him, her eyes full of mistrust and fear.

"I wasn't sure I should come. I don't even know you. Maybe I'm out of my mind."

"You're not out of your mind. You shouldn't trust me, or anyone really. Even if you leave on your way tomorrow and never give me another glance, I'm just glad that you got away from those people." David shook his head in disgust as he thought of Henry even though he had never laid eyes on him.

"They're not all bad. I loved being Amish." Hannah looked defensive all of a sudden and David scolded himself internally.

"Then why? I mean in your letters you said that they weren't going to give you a choice and they weren't talking about it or something." David felt confused. What had this girl been talking about if not her fellow community?

"There are bad people in every community. There is always someone who won't listen or who doesn't want to look closer. It doesn't really have anything to do with me being Amish." Hannah shrugged her shoulders.

David nodded his head in understanding. He certainly knew of a few bad eggs, himself included. He shouldn't have this Amish young woman here. She was too kind and innocent to be around the likes of him.

"So, what next?" Hannah asked. From her look, David assumed that it wasn't the first time she had asked it.

"Next, I figured you could take a train trip up north. You'll be away from Henry, who I'm assuming you are running from."

Hannah nodded.

"Can I ask why?" David wanted to kick himself as soon as he said the words. Of course, she wouldn't want to talk a about why she was running away. She probably thought she had shared too much already through his unauthorized reading of her letters.

"I don't want to get into it, but let's just say he doesn't respect a woman. What he does know is how to use his fist."

David clenched his jaw. He knew a few men like that, and they didn't belong having a woman.

Instead of voicing his opinion on the manner, he just nodded grimly. He felt all the happier that he had gotten her out of that situation.

"If I went up north, who would I stay with?"

"I haven't figured that part out yet, but if you would trust me, I could go with you and we could figure it out together."

Hannah's face filled with even more distrust. "What do you have to run away from? It looks like you have a good life here, with your father, didn't you say?"

"Not exactly. Even though we both live here my father and I don't really get along. In fact, I could really use a break from this whole place. If you would like, I'll leave it all behind." David paused, "But if you don't trust me, and don't want me along, I understand and will set you on your way alone."

Hannah chewed on her lower lip. "Let me get a good night's sleep and we can talk about it in the morning."

David nodded and left the room. He heard the door close softly behind him. Now all he could do was hope that Hannah would give him a chance to prove himself and to start over, he certainly knew he didn't deserve it, but it would be the best gift he could possibly receive.

—-*—-

- Six Months Later

Hannah watched the scenery outside the train window passing her by just like the last three months had passed, much too fast.

She glanced over to where David was sleeping. They had been on the train together for so long now, she could hardly remember what her life was like without him.

He had proven that he was trustworthy, kind and honest. If Hannah was being honest with herself, she was falling in love with him.

She gave a little smile as he began to wake up. "Where are we?" he asked groggily rubbing his eyes.

"We're almost there." Hannah scooted over so that David could look out the window.

"I know it might not seem like it right now, but I do believe I'm going to miss being on the train."

Hannah giggled, "A month ago I would have said that I could never possibly miss this train, but I know what you mean."

The two of them looked out at the snow-capped trees that looked colder than ice.

"Hannah, I know that I've told you this in a way before, but I want you to know before we move on with our lives that I love you and I hope that we'll stick together."

Hannah felt her heart beat faster. The last time someone had said that he had died. The day on the river with Mark came rushing back to her. He had been out there because of her, and he had fallen into the river when she had returned his feelings and he had moved unexpectedly in their boat.

For a moment, Hannah felt her heart constrict with fear, but she forced herself to breathe. This wasn't a river, and Mark wasn't here any longer.

This was David. The man she had come to love. The man who had protected her when she had needed it most.

She smiled, "I love you too, David. Don't you dare think of going off alone. You promised to show me how to get started up here in the north."

David grinned ear to ear and Hannah knew she was exactly where she belonged.

AMISH VALLEY

MICHELLE BENTON

January

You have to stop this! Naomi chided herself, trying to silence what was happening in her head. But she could not stop her foot from tapping and her neck from bopping as she hummed under her breath. *Someone is going to catch you one day and then you'll have some explaining to do.*

She kept her head down so she would not be heard laughing. However, her snickers did not fall on deaf ears and when she turned her head from the firewood she was splitting, two of the women glared at her from their various vegetables.

"Do you find something amusing, Naomi?" Anke Hilty asked coldly but Naomi quickly shook her head and averted her eyes. Still, she could not stop the smile from toying on her generous mouth. She had only been welcomed into the district four months earlier but it seemed that Naomi was still regarded as Englisch to several of the women in the community. Naomi was smart enough to realize that it had little to do with her personally and more to do with upsetting tradition but it did not ease her sense of discomfort. Women like Anke and Anke's sister, Emma made the conversion to the Amish way of life difficult sometimes. If not for Naomi's unstoppable sense of humor, she was sure she would have returned to life in Indianapolis long ago. *I'll be an outsider until I get baptized,* she reasoned, turning her attention fully toward the garden now and forcing any other "English" thought from her head...like the popular song which had been playing over and over in her mind since she had woken at dawn.

"Naomi, you can't be serious!" her mother had screamed when Naomi had told of her plans to convert. "You can't go a day without the internet!"

Naomi had shaken her head, expecting the histrionics from her mother, inwardly relieved to know she would not have to listen to the woman's incessant shrieking day in and day out.

"I can and I will."

"We won't be able to visit you!" her father had protested. "They don't allow for outsiders in their community."

"I know! Isn't it wonderful?" As Naomi spoke, she genuinely meant the words. The Amish way of life, their seclusion, their devotion to each other and God was inspirational to her in every conceivable way.

But it had been Stephen who had almost made her change her mind.

"You can't run away from your problems by disappearing, sis," he told her. "You will just find yourself walking into a whole new whack of problems. But if this is what you want to do, I support you, no matter what. I hope you know I'll miss you."

His words had hit a sour note with Naomi and that night and every night subsequently, what he had said had rung in her head. *I am not running away,* she told herself over and over. *I am trying to under-complicate my very overcomplicated life. It is too messy now, filled with things I do not require. All I need is to surround myself with fresh air, hard work and true, unpretentious, like minded people.* She knew that her family was concerned about her mental state. Ever since her fiancé, Carlos had fled town with her best friend, things had begun to spiral downhill for Naomi. In the aftermath of the betrayal, she had set fire to all his belongings during an onset of uncontrollable fury. She had done so on the front lawn of the house they shared, hoping that Carlos would return and see a pile of ash where his beloved Gucci ties had once been. Carlos had never shown his face at the house again and unfortunately, the act had resulted in an arrest as the flame had spread, damaging the neighbor's car. She had been lucky, let off on probation as it was a first offense and then promptly fired from her job as a personal support worker.

"I'm sorry, Arry, I really am," her boss had told her, regret gleaming in his eyes. "But you can't have an arson record and work with the public, especially not in the medical field."

"I've been working here for four years! It was a stupid act of passion!" Naomi had protested, tears threatening to flow down her round cheeks as her full mouth quivered. "I am no danger to anyone!"

"I know that, Arry and you know that but you know you are required to have a clean record. I can't keep you employed with this agency any more." As he led her away in full blown sobs, he emptily promised to give her an excellent reference but he knew just as well as she did that no one was ever going to hire her again as a PSW. A felony was a felony after all. From there, she had been evicted as she wallowed in depression, eating ice cream and watching Netflix twenty hours a day. Naomi had not a cent in savings and between asking her parents for money and living on the streets, Naomi opted for the latter. She went to stay with Stephen for a short time before having an epiphany one day at the farmer's market; she would join the Amish. At the start, even she had recognized how obscure an idea it was but it did not stop her from investigating. She began frequenting the market more often, discovering that it was almost unheard of for outsiders to convert. Naomi pushed the issue, finding only two people who would entertain her questions. One was a man named Camp Girod, a solemn faced farmer who answered her inquiries in as few words as possible but Naomi soon learned that was his way of speaking and not rudeness. The other was Emma Hilty, a girl who had promised to become a fruitful friendship but had somehow fallen short down the line. Both had seemed happy that she had shown so much interest in their faith and were eager to educate her to the best of their ability. One afternoon, Camp brought the bishop of their district to meet with Naomi to answer some things they did not know. Naomi had almost hugged the tall, shy man but immediately stopped herself. *You must behave like a proper Amish woman from here on in,* Naomi told herself. *No more city girl shenanigans.*

The bishop initially had not been convinced by Naomi but as time went on, he began to recognize her intentions as true and slowly, with

Camp and Emma whispering praise in his ear, he eventually began to take her seriously.

"It is often very difficult for an outsider to simply assimilate into our culture. We don't have the luxuries which your kind seem to deem necessity to function," the Bishop had warned. "More often than not, the English return to the life in which they have been reared."

"That won't happen with me, Bishop!" Naomi declared with conviction. "I will be one hundred and twenty-five percent committed to the community. You'll see!"

The elderly man had raised a bushy eyebrow, somewhat distastefully at Naomi's loud proclamation.

"Naomi, in our community, patience and peace are considered large attributes. The quick tempered and moody do not fare well in our lifestyle," Bishop Kurtz continued. "We are one with God's teaching and he teaches the virtues of the meek. Do you believe you can follow those teachings?"

Naomi nodded eagerly although inwardly she cringed at her own lie. In truth, she had little religious teachings and knew very little about the Bible. She vowed that she would read the scripture from start to finish. *I'll do it in one sitting if that's what it takes!* In the end, Bishop Kurtz decided that Naomi would try the Amish way, largely influenced by Camp and Emma's convincing but partially enthralled by her belief that she was meant to be Amish. Under normal circumstances, the Bishop would not have entertained such an inane idea but Naomi had become a legend in the district and he had finally allowed his curiosity to get the best of him. Every evening after market, one of the parishioners would regale the bishop of tales. A young, bubbly woman would stop by their stalls at the market, begging for information about their culture. Most dismissed her, believing her to be a reporter and not wishing to fraternize with outsiders or disclose anything inappropriate. However, Emma had been amused by her tenacity and began to converse with the girl. She had been pleasantly surprised to discover that Naomi had a genuine desire to forsake the outside world and start fresh within the security of their community. Before long, Camp Girod, whose dairy booth neighbored Emma's meat display, heard the outgoing Naomi and found himself drawn into conversations also. If Emma and Camp had not been such upstanding members of the district, Bishop Kurtz would have never met Naomi Pryce. In the end, however, he was just as smitten with the girl as the other two members of his parish.

On a warm night in September, Naomi, in only a very simple skirt and white blouse, said good bye to Indianapolis and moved into the Hilty's home in rural Indiana with Bishop Kurtz's blessing.

That had been four months earlier. In that time, Emma had lost her good nature with Naomi. Naomi suspected it had much to do with the fact that Anke did not like her. Naomi tried to tell herself it did not matter, that she belonged there just as much as they did. *Just because I wasn't born into this life, doesn't make me any less Amish!* She pep talked herself. At that moment, another popular song blasted into her head. She shook her head mournfully. *My own psyche is mocking me.*

"It's raining on your head, Naomi and yet you seem so content, sitting there in the mud." Naomi whipped her head up and looked at the speaker. Anke and Emma's brother Evan stood above her, his light blue eyes twinkling with laughter. To her surprise, she realized he was right. The sunlight had disappeared and dark rain clouds had overtaken the sky. She suddenly realized that the Hilty sisters had retreated inside without saying a word. Water was seeping into her boots and the air had taken on a sudden chill. She rubbed her hands against her

"Come inside before you fall ill," Evan laughed, offering a hand. She eagerly accepted and followed the oldest Hilty sibling inside the farmhouse. Anke scowled at them from the window and Naomi realized she was still holding Evan's hand. Embarrassed, she pulled her palm from his and he turned, winking at her. Naomi blushed crimson. Evan had bestowed endless attention upon her since her arrival in the district. From the first night, he had told her stories on the porch and introduced her around to the neighbors. In turn, he asked that she tell him about the city, the sights and people. Naomi did her best to make it sound exciting, despite her recollection being less than glamorous but it seemed the more she embellished, the more captivated Evan became. Naomi had almost felt like he had claimed her but of course that was ridiculous. That was something the English would do, not the gentle-minded Amish. Still, Naomi was flattered and relished the friendship she found in Evan.

"Let me make some tea. You should change your clothes. I don't understand how you can be so at peace in the rain," Evan told her. "Especially someone so accustom to having warmth at their fingertips!"

Naomi shrugged. It was difficult not to be at peace in such surroundings. There was no bustle, no stress. The days were long, yes, but Naomi felt as if she had always been tilling fields and saying prayers. She hadn't been certain that the religious aspect would appeal to her, being reared nearly agnostic but the more time she had spent in worship, hearing God's plans, the more Naomi recognized what she had been missing from her life. *You made the right choice coming here,* she told herself as she quickly changed and brushed out her dark hair. She regarded her reflection in the mirror. She was an attractive woman by any standards; shoulder length straight brown hair, her bangs finally growing out from the blunt cut she had worn from before joining the community. Her dark eyes were intelligent and wide, her mouth constantly curved to a smile. Her inner happiness radiated outwardly and she found herself smiling in the glass.

"Are you coming?" Evan bellowed from downstairs. "The tea is becoming cold!"

"Yes!" Naomi yelled back and winced. *You need to tone it down!*

She hurried out of her small room and down the stairs to meet with Evan in the kitchen. Emma stopped her, stepping out from the shadows in the sitting room.

"Naomi," she said in a low voice. Naomi paused in surprise, glancing toward the kitchen but Evan was not standing there.

"You need to stay away from my brother," she warned. "Don't say I didn't warn you." Naomi felt her heart skip a beat. In the darkness of the hall, Naomi thought she saw a glint of anger in the younger girl's eyes. She did not reply, instead backing away, looking hurt at Emma's words, watching the younger girl disappear up the stairs. *I suppose I am not good enough for her brother, then? Am I always going to be an outsider? Will they never accept me here?*

"Naomi, would you care to take a walk with me after supper tomorrow?" Camp asked conversationally after worship. Naomi nodded.

"Of course," she replied, unsuspectingly. "I would love to!"

"There is a matter I would like to discuss with you," he said in his usual somber tone. Naomi smiled to herself but nodded again. She could not imagine Camp being anything but serious. *He probably wants to discuss the winter frost and he makes it sound like the world is about to come to an end,* she thought jokingly. She dared not jest with Camp. He was far too routine for such play. Naomi had once been present when Camp had been unwell and overslept as a result. She had never seen anyone so flustered in all her life. His entire demeanor had been altered and he snapped viciously at everyone in his wake. Naomi had been wounded by his sharp tones until Emma had told her that Camp was the most structured person in their district. From the time he was a child, he had risen with the roosters and planned every single minute of every day down to the second. When his schedule was disrupted, it made him confused and disoriented. After learning that, Naomi had gone out of her way to accommodate his whims. After all, if it had not been for Camp, she likely would never have been allowed in the community. Naomi owed him a debt of gratitude. Also, Camp was one of her only friends. She didn't know why, but Camp seemed to like her.

"You're not like anyone I would ever imagine Camp Giron associating," Anke told Naomi icily one day after Camp walked away. Naomi and he had been speaking over the fence for almost half an hour. Naomi had raised an eyebrow, stung by the connotation.

"And why not?" she demanded. "I am just as God fearing and hard working as anyone here, Anke! I wish you wouldn't imply that I'm not!"

"Maybe so," the older sister had replied. "But you are also the loudest. Camp is a quiet, gentle man. You are so...brash."

"Brash? I am not brash!" Naomi had yelled. Anke had smiled thinly as if to say "I rest my case." Naomi had gone out of her way to avoid speaking with Anke after that but Anke made it easy. She barely had two words to say to Naomi under the best of circumstances. Inwardly, though, she wondered what Camp found interesting about her. *Anke is not wrong. I am exactly the opposite of the man. I always thought that introverts found extroverts exhausting.* Naomi did not have to wait long to find out.

The following evening, the night had turned bitterly cold but after supper, Camp knocked on the Hilty door. Naomi hurried threw on her coat, scarf and gloves before adjusting her bonnet and heading toward the front door to meet her friend. Evan grabbed her by the arm as she went to leave the kitchen, a scowl darkening his fair face.

"Are you going out walking with Camp Giron?" he demanded. Surprised, Naomi nodded at the question.

"Yes," she answered, cocking her head in confusion. Evan's blue eyes narrowed dangerously.

"Is that a problem?" Naomi asked nervously. She studied his face for an answer and suddenly he realized how tightly he was holding her. Abruptly, he let her go, shame flooding his face.

"No, of course not," he told her hastily. "I – it's very cold outside is all. Please dress well." With that he disappeared into the back of the house, leaving Naomi staring after him, open mouthed. *Am I delusional or was that an act of jealousy?* She asked herself, a warm glow of happiness filling her insides. She had suspected that Evan liked her but he had never been anything more than friendly toward her even though the community called his ways flirty. She secretly hoped that he was jealous of Camp. She pushed Evan out of her mind as she remembered that Camp was waiting for her. *You must not make Camp wait,* she thought guiltily but Camp did not look perturbed as he stood in the foyer, chatting with Mrs. Hilty.

"Ah, there you are, Naomi. Please do not be late. We have a very busy morning tomorrow," the matriarch ordered and Naomi nodded obligingly. Naomi had never given the Hilty's any cause for alarm. She had done everything per her agreement with Bishop Kurtz.

"Remember, Naomi," Bishop Kurtz had told her when she had arrived. "It is not what I expect of you but what God and this community expect of you. You will see a reflection of yourself in every action, good or bad. The choice is yours but in the end, it is only you who must answer to God."

"Shall we?" Camp extended his arm and Naomi took it, smiling. The pathway to the road was icy and Camp held fast to her as she almost slipped several times.

"My goodness, Camp," Naomi exclaimed as ten minutes had only seen them a few hundred feet down the road. "Perhaps we should plan our walk for another night."

"I would prefer not to, Naomi if you do not mind indulging me." Naomi smiled and shrugged tolerantly. She could barely feel her face or toes in the extreme cold but she did not want to disappoint Camp.

"This sounds urgent, Camp. Of course, we can speak tonight. What is going on?"

Camp paused and looked down at her, his own dark eyes soulfully deep. He seemed to be thinking about his words and in spite of her resolve to be patient, Naomi wished he would spit it out. She flexed her fingers inside her gloves to ensure they were still there.

"Naomi, I am very proud of the way you have situated yourself in the community," he began. She smiled, abashed by the praise.

"I couldn't have done it without you, Camp. You know that, right?"

"I believe that your perseverance would have paid off regardless of my small role. However, I am happy you are here."

"I am thrilled to be here!" she announced. He nodded soberly and cocked his head.

"Have you given any thought to your baptism?" he questioned.

"Bishop Kurtz has suggested April. Personally, I would like to do it tomorrow but I confess, I never much wanted to join the Polar Bear Club." A look of confusion passed over Camp's eyes and Naomi realized he didn't understand the reference. *You really need to get your head out of the English,* she scolded herself again.

"Anyway, you'll know when I know. I'm pretty sure everyone around here gets an invite, right? Is that what you want to talk about? You're worried I might go back to the city after everything you've done to bring me here?" she asked, smiling. Camp's brow furrowed and Naomi realized that he had not entertained that thought whatsoever, at least not until she had brought it up.

"No..." he said slowly. "That was not what I wanted to speak to you regarding."

He said nothing and Naomi felt a smidgen of annoyance. *I know patience is a virtue but I'm becoming an ice sculpture here!*

"Camp, you're my friend, you know that, right?" He nodded, seemingly more confused by the conversation shift.

"As my friend, probably my best friend here, I am begging you to ask me whatever it is because I am freezing to death! I swear there are corpses warmer than me right now!"

Camp inhaled sharply and nodded.

"I wanted to ask you, if, once you get baptized..."

"Yes?"

"If you would consider giving me your hand in marriage?"

<u>**April**</u>

"Welcome, Naomi Pryce to our community!"

A cheer erupted and Naomi, soaked to her knickers, beamed at the crowd which surrounded her. She noted with pride that even Anke nodded in approval, a thin, funny smile pursing her lips. *I am one of them now! Finally! They can't call me an outsider anymore!* She thought. She turned to Bishop Kurtz and bowed slightly in thanks.

"We are pleased to have you, Naomi. You have demonstrated the loyalty, hard work and patience which we value so highly. If only you would work on your Pennsylvania Dutch..." A small chuckle flew through the group and Evan lunged forward to take her arm.

"Everyone speaks English anyway, *liebchen*. Come on, Arry. Let's eat!" Happily, she allowed herself to be led toward the Hilty barn where a feast had been set up for the baptism. Out of the corner of her eye, she saw Camp standing alone, under a tree, looking forlorn.

Since the frigid night of their walk, Camp had not come calling and Naomi admitted that she missed his company terribly. Of course, Evan was her constant companion, joking and laughing with her, despite the tongue wagging of the community.

"She does not behave properly," some of the older women complained. "She flirts recklessly with the Hilty boy and she lives in that house!"

"He is no better," others countered. "He has been brought up right in this community and he blatantly disregards our traditions. He acts like he has English blood."

But neither Evan or Naomi seemed to mind the gossip. It was not because they did not hear of it; in fact, Mr. and Mrs. Hilty often forbade them to be together alone but they still managed to find a way to see one another and enjoy each other's company. Naomi had been counting the days to her christening. She knew that the moment she officially became Amish, Evan would ask her to marry. *I wonder if he will do it today even,* Naomi thought, peering at him out of the corner of her eye. He returned her look of adoration and impulsively squeezed her hand, not releasing it. Naomi did not take her palm away this time, despite the looks she received from the members. She could almost hear their thoughts; *she just got accepted into the fold and look at her! Acting like a fallen woman!* Naomi did not care. She was incredibly happy and she knew she was about to become happier.

The day progressed beautifully. There was food and banter. The only dark cloud was Camp's almost palpable sadness. She had not outright refused his pre-emptive proposal but she had let him down in a way that he knew she did not see a future with him. *Camp will find someone. He is dependable and hardworking. Any woman in the community would be lucky to have him.* But the thoughts did not alleviate Naomi's guilt and she forced herself to focus on the festivities. As the afternoon wound into evening, she found herself exhausted. The events of the day had taken a toll on her and she wanted to retire early for the evening. She excused herself just after dark and retreated to her bedroom. As she lay in bed, a smile touching her lips, she knew that tomorrow would be the day Evan would ask her to marry him.

"Naomi!" She bolted up in her bed, scared out of a dream state. It took her a moment to reconcile her surroundings and then, through the dark, she peered at Emma and Anke who stood in the doorway, both relief and anger written on their faces.

"What?" she croaked, her throat like cotton. "What happened?"

Emma exhaled slowly and crept into the dark room, clutching a letter in her hand.

"You're still here."

"Well I almost jumped out of my skin but yes, I am still here. What is going on?" Naomi demanded, throwing her legs over the side of the twin bed and rubbing her eyes.

"We thought you had gone with him," Anke answered crisply, also entering the room. She snatched the paper out of Emma's hand and flung it at Naomi.

"Gone with who? Guys, it's a little early in the morning for brain teasers. Can you tell me what is happening or can I go back to bed?"

"Do you know anything about this?"

Naomi picked up the single sheet of paper and read the note scrawled on the blank canvas.

Dear *Daed, Mammi,* Anke and Emma,

You have always done your best for me but I have never felt like I belonged in this community. I think I always knew that I would leave at some point but it wasn't until Naomi came that I knew the world was calling me. I could not stop thinking about the places she told me, the foods she had eaten, the people she met. I could not understand why she would give that all up to live here, in this boring, judgemental place. I have gone to the city. Don't worry about me, please. I am sure I will make my way just fine. I know this comes as a disappointment but I could not bear the thought of spending my life farming. I love you all.

Yours Always,

Evan

P.S. Tell Naomi if she changes her mind to come and find me in Indianapolis.

Slowly, Naomi read and reread the letter until tears began to slip down her cheeks and blot the ink on the paper. Anke grabbed it and swatted the water from the page scowling.

"*Mamm* and *Daed* haven't read it yet, Naomi. Don't ruin it. You've already ruined enough around here." Anke spun on her heel and stormed out the door, leaving Emma behind. The younger sister looked at Naomi's devastated face and gently placed her hand upon her shoulder.

"I told you to stay away from Evan," she murmured. "Not because you're not good enough for him but because he is not good enough for you."

<u>**May**</u>

"Naomi, you have been moping around here for a month now. I miss your sunny smile," Bishop Kurtz told her one day as he passed by the farm.

"I am not moping, Bishop!" Naomi protested. "I am working!"

"Yes, yes you are working and doing a fine job, I might add," he agreed. "But you need to forget about Evan. I understand you were very fond of him."

"He was my friend." Naomi dropped the hoe and stared at the bishop. The look was enough to stop him from uttering his next thoughts but his eyes travelled over her head to look at something in the distance.

"Well, I still miss your smile, child," he told her. "And sometimes when God closes a door, he opens up a window." She followed his gaze as he turned to leave and she saw Camp approaching in a wagon.

"Good day, Naomi," Camp greeted, somewhat nervously. "Would you care to go for a ride? I have an appointment with a medical doctor in town today."

Immediately, Naomi was concerned.

"Are you all right?" she asked, hurrying forward, wiping her dirty hands on her apron.

"Oh yes. Nothing serious. But I wouldn't mind the company," he replied. Naomi nodded quickly. *It is serious enough for him to ask her for companionship after an estrangement*, she thought nervously.

"Just give me a minute to change."

She was beside him in the carriage in minutes and they rode silently for a while.

"Naomi, when are you going to stop brooding about?"

"I am not brooding!" she snapped. *I'm not brooding! I am pining. Evan could come back any day. That is not brooding or moping. That is called being hopeful.*

"Fine." They continued their trip quietly. Naomi realized how unfair she was being to Camp. Camp was there. Evan was not. Camp stood by her. Evan hadn't even asked if she wanted to go with him. Why would she not give Camp a chance?

"I'm sorry, Camp," she finally said. He shot her a look out of the corner of his eye.

"What for?"

"I don't deserve your affections. You have been too good to me since the beginning."

"You are very worthy of all things good, Naomi. It has been my pleasure you call you my friend."

Naomi looked at him, his noble face proud and unsmiling.

"Would it be your pleasure to call me your wife?"

October

When their engagement was announced at worship, Naomi was met with genuine adulation.

"Camp Giron is a fine man. He will be Bishop one day, I promise you. You have made the right decision," Bishop Kurtz told her. "And I do believe you have made the man very happy. I have known Camp since he was a boy. I could count the amount of times he has smiled on one hand since then. Until you came along, Naomi. He adores you."

"He is a wonderful man," Naomi agreed, shooting her fiancé a look from across the salon. He met her gaze and smiled. Bishop Kurtz opened his mouth to say something else but seemed to reconsider.

"I hope you two will be very happy together, Naomi."

"I hope so too," she replied, a sudden stab of sadness overwhelming her. She would be lying to herself to say she didn't still think of Evan. She wondered if he was faring well in the city and if he ever thought about her. She knew that he wasn't coming back.

"He would not be welcome here if he did," Anke spat when Naomi asked her about him one night. Naomi had been shocked at the venom attached to his sister's words. Later, Emma pulled her aside.

"I know you were rather fond of my brother," Emma told her. "But there are many things you did not know about him."

Naomi arched an eyebrow. She wasn't sure she wanted to hear anything negative about Evan but curiosity got the better of her.

"Such as?" But Emma pursed her lips together as if she had already said too much.

"Just believe me, Naomi. You are marrying a good man in Camp. He will always do right by you." The words meant little to Naomi who lay awake at night, listening for sounds, dreaming that Evan would sneak back into the house and into her life again.

November

"You are a lovely bride," Emma whispered, adjusting the wreath of flowers about Naomi's head. Naomi smiled genuinely and gave her a hug.

"I don't think I've ever thanked you for all you've done for me, Emma," she told the younger girl. The blonde blinked and looked confused.

"What have I done?"

"You have helped give me a sense of community and family, one I have never had. I know you don't think I belong here but I want you to know that I care more about these people and our way of life than anyone or anything I have before in my life."

"I know you belong here, Naomi. That is why I asked Bishop Kurtz to speak with you. Camp and I saw the purity in your soul from the first day we met you. You are exactly the kind of person we want walking among us." The women smiled at each other and for the first time since Evan had left, Naomi felt truly happy. *I do belong here. I am one of them. Thanks to Emma and Bishop Kurtz. And thanks to Camp.*

"Shall we?" Emma offered Naomi her arm and the two made their way into the church where Camp stood waiting at the altar. Naomi felt like she was seeing him for the first time. He looked so handsome, his dark hair shining under his hat, two glossy curls hanging about his chiseled features. His eyes were alight with adoration as he watched his bride to be slowly walk toward him. His face broke into a beam so broad, Naomi was sure his face would crack from the force. Tears misted his irises. Emma gently squeezed her arm and released toward Camp. Suddenly, an abrupt gust of wind flew through the small chapel, extinguishing several of the lamps. Bride and groom turned toward the entrance where a form stood, panting in the opened doorway.

"Evan!" Naomi gasped. Immediately, Mr. Hilty rose to his feet, his face crimson in anger.

"How dare you show your face in here!" he thundered.

"I am not here for you, *Daed*," Evan retorted, his eyes remaining on Naomi as he stumbled up the aisle.

"Naomi, don't marry him!" he called as he approached. "Come back to the city with me. I made a mistake leaving you here but you're all I can think about." A murmur flowed through the crowd. *He did think about me! He does miss me!* Naomi thought, dumbfounded. Evan was at the altar, grabbing for her hands, his blue eyes pleading.

"I'm sorry! I made a mistake," he said again, his mouth turning up into a smile of contrition. Naomi glanced up at Camp, who had lost the rare beam which had lit up the church. She looked at Emma who shook her head woefully and stared at her shoed. Her gaze shifted to Bishop Kurtz whose mouth had formed a fine line. She stared into the crowd and took in Evan's family's look of shame and fury. Then she looked back at Camp again.

"I'm sorry," she whispered at him and Camp hung his head in defeat, his shoulders visibly sagging. Evan tightened his grip on her hands and Naomi yanked them back, her eyes still trained on Camp.

"I am sorry," she said again, reaching up to wipe the tears falling onto his cheeks. "I am sorry that I ever made you hurt. I am so sorry that I wasted any time on this man. I am so terribly sorry that I ever doubted my future is in your arms. I love you, Camp." She turned furiously to Evan who had gone pale at Naomi's speech.

"But Naomi – "

"What kind of disgusting man claims to love a woman and leaves her for months only to barge in on her wedding? You're despicable, Evan. And you're not welcome in our community – my community! Get out and don't return." After a stunned second of silence, Evan whirled on his heel and ran out the door.

"And you don't even close the door behind you! Can you imagine marrying such a man?" Naomi yelled after him. Applause and laughter broke out and someone hurried to shut the double doors and relight the kerosene lamps. Naomi took Camp's hands in hers and they gazed into each other's eyes lovingly.

"Now, where were we?" she asked Bishop Kurtz without looking away.

END

KAYLA

MONICA MARKS

It was Kayla's favorite time of year and when she woke that morning, she inhaled deeply, absorbing the nostalgic feeling which the onset of autumn brought along.

It is time for harvest and engagement announcements, she thought happily, swinging her long legs off the single mattress and scurrying to the window to stare into to endless farmland. The smallest frost had settled overnight but there was no cause for concern; the sunshine was fighting to warm the October day already and it was just past dawn. She tried to ignore the near exhaustion in her bones and stretched, willing herself to wake up.

I slept more than enough, she reasoned with her weary body. *There is no reason for me to be so tired.*

She told herself that the crisp fall air would invigorate her.

"Kayla!"

Her younger sister, Hannah threw open the door to her bedroom and folded her small arms across her chest.

"Haven't you dressed yet? It is almost seven o'clock!"

"Haven't you learned to knock yet? You are almost eight years old," Kayla replied haughtily. The sisters stared at each other before bursting into laughter.

"I am coming, Hannah," she assured the child. "There is time for breakfast and to walk to school."

Hannah smiled and Kayla clapped her hands.

"You lost another tooth!" she declared, rushing forward to examine her sister's mouth. "Let me see."

Hannah opened her mouth obligingly and the older sister patted her cheek.

"Go show *Daed* now," she instructed. "I will be along in a moment."

Hannah turned to leave Kayla, rushing down the steps toward the kitchen and Kayla hurried to change.

Hannah was not wrong; she had slept in again. It seemed to be happening with more frequency and Kayla had first believed the change of weather had been affecting her but suddenly she was not so certain.

I must eat better, she chided herself, slipping into a dark brown work dress and fastening an apron atop her skirt. *Autumn is not the time to waste time sleeping when Daed needs help with harvest and winter preparations. If you are so tired when the days are still long, what will you be like in two months?*

She padded across the threshold and into the corridor, trying to recall what needed to be done that morning. Canning needed to be started, the hay baled, pickling, jams...the list was endless as always and Kayla began to form a list in her mind in order of importance.

Slipping down the stairs, Kayla was suddenly overwhelmed by a wave of dizziness. She clutched the bannister, blood draining from her face as she tried to gather her bearings.

Oh Gotte, I do not have the luxury of being sick, she warned herself, willing a feeling of normalcy to come but in seconds, her legs had buckled and to her horror, Kayla tumbled down the remaining three steps onto the landing.

Not again! She thought, horrified, knowing that her family would witness her embarrassment this time. It was the third fainting spell she had experienced in two weeks but gratefully, her father and sister had not seen the others.

As spots of black and red danced before her eyes, she opened her mouth to moan but she began to lose consciousness as Hannah came running into the foyer, their father in tow.

The last thing she recalled before the world went dark was her small sister screaming.

When she woke, Jeremiah Roth stood praying over her, his eyes closed but even without reading the expression in his gentle blue irises, Kayla could see the concern in his face.

"*Daed*?" she called weakly, struggling to sit up against the bed. She realized she had been put back in her room, tucked in snugly among blankets.

"Oh, Kayla!" Jeremiah gasped, his lids flying open at the sound of her voice. "You must remain still. I have asked the Fishers to call for Dr. Imhoff."

"I am fine, *Daed*," Kayla protested. "It was nothing, I am sure. It happens sometimes."

"How many times?" Jeremiah demanded, his cornflower blue eyes wide with shock. "Why did you not tell me before?"

"It is no cause for alarm. Cancel the doctor!" Kayla groaned.

"Hush, *liebchen*," he insisted, pointing at the bed. "You will remain here until the doctor has seen you."

"We haven't time for this," Kayla insisted, attempting to rise again. "We have much to do."

"I am your father," Jeremiah growled with uncharacteristic sternness. "You will do as you are told. The harvest can wait."

Kayla settled back, blinking.

"All right, *Daed*," she relented. "I will wait but the Dr. Imhoff will tell you there is nothing wrong."

"I would rather hear it from him," Jeremiah replied. "He is the one with the medical degree after all."

He turned to the bedside and produced a glass of water.

"Drink this. I will wait downstairs Jonah."

"Where is Hannah?"

"Lydia Fisher has taken her to school. You mustn't worry, Kayla. All is tended to this morning. Your job is to rest."

He turned to leave the room before Kayla could form another argument, leaving her to stare at the ceiling is mild exasperation.

This is foolish, she thought but she dared not express her feelings aloud. She knew her father was concerned and she had no one to blame but herself.

I have been neglecting meals and sleeping poorly, she chided herself. *Now I have worried everyone.*

In minutes, she heard footfalls on the stairs and the door opened.

"*Guter mayire*, Kayla," Dr. Imhoff announced, smiling in his kindly way. "I understand you had a small fainting episode this morning."

Kayla stifled a sigh.

"It was nothing," she insisted.

"I will see about that," Jonah Imhoff replied lightly, opening his bag.

He checked her eyes and throat, running her temperature and pinching her skin to test for validity.

Then he turned to Jeremiah.

"We will talk outside," he told the patriarch, patting Kayla's face warmly.

"You should rest today, Kayla," he told her, closing his bag. Kayla chewed on her tongue to keep a thousand objections from erupting and watched helplessly as the men retreated into the hallway.

She strained her ears to listen, catching only a few words as she did.

"...tests...color...must be vigilant."

Their voices cut in and out but Kayla felt a prickle slide down her back as she understood the gist of their conversation.

He believes there is something wrong with me, she realized, concern floating through her for the first time since the incidents had begun. She tried to dismiss the feeling of worry but when her father returned to the bedroom, his eyes shone with something she had not seen in many years.

"Jonah is arranging for you to have tests done at Lancaster General Hospital," he told her gravely. Kayla swallowed quickly, realizing there was a lump in her throat.

"What does he believe is wrong, *Daed*?" she whispered and Jeremiah seemed to recognize his mistake, wiping the dismayed frown from his face.

"Nothing specific, *liebchen,*" he replied quickly. "It is merely a precaution. Do not fret; we will learn what ails you soon enough."

"*Daed,* I am certain it is - "

"You are not a doctor, Kayla. In the meanwhile, you will rest. I will see if Lydia can stay with you while I tend to the farm," he continued and Kayla heard no room for debate in his tone.

"*Daed*, you cannot tend the farm alone," she sighed. "You would better have Lydia help you."

Jeremiah stared at her for a long while as if he was looking directly through her.

"You are correct," he told her softly. "I must enlist help until you are better."

Without another word, he spun and walked from the bedroom, leaving Kayla to stare after him with her mouth agape in question.

The wagon drew near the farmhouse, Lydia Fisher leading the horse through the grey day. They were returning from Kayla's appointment at the hospital where she had undergone bloodwork for her ever increasing fainting and general fatigue.

"Would you like me to come with you, Kayla?" Lydia asked as she slid from the bench onto the dirt. Kayla stifled a sigh and shook her head, forcing a smile onto her lips. She was growing tired of being coddled by both her father and the neighbors, despite their good intentions.

"I feel fine," she fibbed. In reality, she wished to lay down but she dared not say anything to Lydia. The last thing she wished to do was cause more of a fuss.

"I will be by later this evening to fix supper for you," Lydia told her, picking up the reins. "Back to bed now."

Kayla did not answer but waved at the butcher's wife as she made her way from the Roth farm toward her own.

I will go mad if I have to spend one more minute in bed, Kayla thought glumly, turning toward the fields. She saw her father in the distance, reaping corn and she longed to run toward him but she did not. She would only interrupt him and take more time from his duties.

Duties I should be tending to also, she told herself, guilt wracking her body.

The doctor at the hospital had been candid with her assessment, citing several reasons for her strange illness.

"But we will run the necessary tests, Kayla and determine the cause."

It was not until Kayla and Lydia were almost home that she realized that the physician had told her nothing of sustenance.

I can only wait for the results – however long that will take. In the meanwhile, Daed is working alone on the farm.

Suddenly, another figure appeared, close to the entrance of the maize and Kayla started.

"Hello!" she called out, her brow furrowing with concern. The stranger turned to look at her and he seemed to freeze as they stared at one another.

"Hello," he replied, turning to face her. Kayla stepped back in surprise as he emerged from the stalks, dressed in pair of blue jeans and a black and red flannel shirt.

"Who are you?" she demanded as she stared at him uncomprehendingly. "Does my father know you are here?"

The dark-haired man paused, cocking his head to the side slightly, a single strand of hair falling directly onto his forehead.

"Yes," he answered. "My name is Will. Will Jenkins."

Kayla waited for him to elaborate on why he stood on their land but he did not speak. Slowly, she drew closer to him.

"Why are you on our land?" Kayla asked, her green eyes narrowing in suspicion. She loathed that she was immediately concerned about the Englisher's presence but she could not reconcile one good reason that the man would be on the property.

"I am helping with the harvest," Will told her simply.

"Helping whom?"

Will stared at her for a long moment as if he was concerned she was slow-witted.

"I am helping the owner of the land obviously," he replied dryly. "Who are you?"

Kayla was reluctant to disclose any information to the man, her eyes lifting to see where her father was in the field.

Daed wouldn't hire an Englisher to help on the farm, she thought, distrustful of Will Jenkins. *And he certainly did not mention bringing on any help.*

To her relief, she was Jeremiah approaching.

"There is my father now," Kayla said sternly. "If you do not belong here, you best run along before he catches you on our property."

Will gave her a bemused smile.

"If I ran along, I would not be doing my job," he told her lightly. "I think your father would be angrier at that."

"Kayla you are home," Jeremiah cried, hurrying toward his daughter. She watched as he glanced nervously at the stranger.

"Come inside and we will talk," the senior Roth said, without acknowledging the Englisher in their midst. Kayla opened her mouth to speak but the look in her father's eye silenced her.

"Yes, *Daed,*" she agreed, turning to follow Jeremiah inside the house. Will remained in place, his mouth upturned and Kayla cast him one long look before entering the house.

"Daed, did you hire that Englisher to help with the harvest?" she asked dubiously.

"Yes, but that is unimportant. Tell me what the doctor said," Jeremiah told her, abruptly changing the conversation.

"But *Daed,* I will be fine soon. You did not need to hire anyone, especially not an outsider!" Kayla cried.

Jeremiah's mouth became a fine line and his eyes narrowed.

"I do not wish to discuss the Englisher," he told her flatly. "I asked you about the doctor. What was said and what tests were done?"

Kayla swallowed another question.

"She believes that it is a blood disorder of sorts but I will not know until the tests come back. Simple bloodwork was performed. I will return next week for the results."

Jeremiah's brow knitted and he nodded.

"What sort of blood disorder?"

Kayla shrugged.

"I do not know, Daed. She did not give me specifics. I can only wait to learn."

Jeremiah did not seem happy with her answer but Kayla had little else to give him.

"Go rest now, Kayla. I will come to you after the work is done."

"*Daed*, may I go for Hannah? I do not wish to spend one more minute in bed. Please?"

Jeremiah regarded her for a long moment before bobbing his head reluctantly.

"If you are certain you are not feeling ill, you may pick up your sister from school. But you must come straight back to bed. Understood?"

Gratefully, Kayla nodded and hurried toward the front door before he could change his mind.

It will be lovely to stretch my legs and inhale the fresh autumn air, she thought. She was beginning to feel as a caged rabbit.

As she walked toward the road, she found herself looking back at Will Jenkins. He was hard at work, paying her no mind but as she turned in the direction of the schoolhouse, Kayla thought she could feel eyes on her.

Who is this man and what is he doing here?

That evening, Lydia Fisher came as promised, preparing a delicious supper for the Roths before heading home to her own family.

"She is a blessing to us," Jeremiah commented when she left and they sat down to eat. Kayla scowled slightly.

"She really doesn't need be here quite so often, *Daed*," she told her father. "I can still work."

"Your health is paramount, Kayla. Lydia has four able sons to work their farm and can spare a hand until you are well."

"I am well!" Kayla grunted, trying to keep the frustration from her voice. Jeremiah shot her a warning look and Kayla clamped her mouth closed. Arguing would not prove fruitful.

"Tell me about the Englisher," Kayla said instead and Hannah's head jerked upward from her stew.

"What Englisher?" the little girl asked curiously. Jeremiah's scowl deepened and he shook his head almost imperceivably at his oldest daughter.

"I have already explained that Will is helping with the harvest. There is nothing else to tell."

"Where did you find him, *Daed*? You must admit that it is odd to bring an outsider here when there are many in the community whom you could call upon for help."

Jeremiah's blue eyes seemed to darken.

"I am the head of this house," he snapped. "I do not need to answer to you for my choices."

Kayla was stung by his tone and she bit her lower lip. It was unlike her father to speak crossly to her or Hannah.

Whatever silliness is happening with me is causing him stress, she determined, taking a spoonful of beef stew. *I must not give him more of a reason to worry.*

She did not mention Will again but she decided that she would speak to Will the next time she saw him and learn more about him.

Kayla had her chance the following day. Jeremiah went to sell their goods at market, leaving Kayla alone.

"I have asked Lydia to come later in the day to ensure you are well," her father told her. Kayla rolled her eyes where he could not see.

You must not get annoyed, she warned herself but she could not help but feel frustrated at being treated like a child. She knew that was not Jeremiah's intention but she could not release the slight resentment she was feeling.

Her mother had died when she was fourteen, leaving Kayla as the woman of the household. Hannah was still an infant and Kayla had learned to tend to both the baby and the farm.

Standing idle was not something which she did well and she wished desperately that the doctors would quickly diagnose her issue so she was able to resume her role in the family and on the farm.

"Thank you, *Daed,*" she said instead of unleashing the barrage of protests vying to spring from her lips.

"I do not want you to leave the house today, Kayla," Jeremiah told her seriously as he stood in the doorway of her bedroom. "Stay inside and preferably in bed. If you are to faint with no one nearby..."

"I will not faint!" she cried but Jeremiah shook his head.

"You have no way of assuring me of that," he replied. "Please heed my words, Kayla. I speak only out of concern for you."

Begrudgingly, Kayla nodded.

"Yes, *Daed,*" she agreed. "I will take Hannah to school and – "

"No," Jeremiah said sharply. "Lydia will take your sister to school."

Kayla gritted her teeth and nodded.

"Have a good day in town, *Daed,*" Kayla sighed. She watched as he retreated to the freshly loaded wagon and disappeared down the road.

I have become a prisoner in my own home, Kayla thought mournfully, folding her arms across her chest. She wondered what she would do for the remainder of the day and as she thought it, she watched a silver sedan car driving up the road which Jeremiah had just taken.

Kayla leaned forward, watching the dilapidated vehicle pull onto their land, her pulse quickening. As she peered at the driver, she realized it was Will Jenkins arriving to work.

Is he supposed to be here today? She wondered nervously. If so, why hadn't her father told her to expect him.

Will jumped from the driver's seat and she noted he was wearing the same clothes he had the day before. He did not seem to notice her observing him, pulling a few items which she could not see from the backseat before turning toward the barn.

As Kayla rose her hand to wave in greeting, something tugged on her skirt.

"Kayla, I am hungry!" Hannah announced from behind her, causing the older girl to jump.

"You startled me, Hannah!" she chided and Hannah shrugged indifferently. She turned to usher her sister into the house, eyeing Will who had vanished behind the house.

I wonder if I should tend to him, she thought but her father's words reverberated in her mind.

"I do not want you to leave the house today, Kayla. Stay inside and preferably in bed. If you are to faint with no one nearby..."

She pushed the thought of Will Jenkins from her mind and closed the door.

She had no reason to approach the Englisher.

The weather had turned unseasonably warm and Kayla lifted her head from her book, realizing that the front room had grown almost stifling hot.

She cast the novel aside and reached to open the window, gazing into the fields. To her surprise, she saw Will Jenkins standing near the maple tree beside his car, wiping sweat from his brow.

Kayla watched him for a moment and she could see the sun and hard work had turned his face red.

He must be thirsty. He is dressed much too warmly to work the fields in that attire, she realized, rising from window seat.

A cool glass of water in hand, Kayla stepped into the yard. Will's back was to her and she tried to make herself heard as to not surprise him.

He turned and Kayla was filled with a strange sense of familiarity suddenly, something she had not felt the previous afternoon.

"Hello," he said and Kayla nodded, handing him the glass of water.

"It is very hot today," she volunteered. "I thought you might be thirsty."

He nodded gratefully and accepted the beverage, drinking it in one long gulp.

"I will fetch you another one," she offered and he shook his head.

"No, thank you," he replied. "I should be getting back to work."

He was older than Kayla with dark hair and vivid green eyes. His face seemed it had not been shaved in four days and there were dark circles under his eyes.

He is handsome in a rugged sort of way, she thought, studying his face. The feeling that she knew him did not diminish.

"As you wish," she replied, turning back.

"Actually wait," Will called nervously. He peered at his gloved hands in embarrassment as Kayla turned back to him.

"Yes?"

"Maybe one more glass of water," he muttered and Kayla smiled.

"Of course."

Inside the house, she thought of the somewhat bedraggled man on her lawn and she again wondered where he had come from.

If he has no water, he likely has no food either, she realized and quickly went to work preparing him a snack. *If he doesn't eat, he will also faint. Daed doesn't need to come home to such a sight.*

She did not want to think what her father would say if he knew she was feeding the Englisher.

Outside, she gestured for him to sit and eat. The gratitude in his face was beyond anything she had ever seen and a mixture of sadness and pity overwhelmed her.

"Are you from Lancaster, Mr. Jenkins?" Kayla asked timidly as he inhaled the bread and cheese she had brought to him. He shook his head and she waited for him to swallow the morsels before answering.

"No," he replied. "I am from Reading."

Kayla's brow furrowed.

"Reading?" she asked in surprise. "You have a little bit of a journey to make here."

Will nodded and shrugged his shoulders.

"It is an hour's drive," he answered. "But your father offered me very good pay and gas money for the trip."

None of what he said made sense to Kayla.

Why would Daed bring an Englisher to the district from an hour away?

"You know, I don't even know your name," Will commented as he polished off the last of the light meal she provided for him.

Embarrassed, Kayla extended her hand.

"Kayla Roth."

Will accepted her outstretched palm and they two looked at one another for a long moment. Kayla felt a sudden confusion as she stared at him.

Why do I feel such an affinity with this man? She wondered, an almost awe-struck feeling overcoming her.

"Nice to meet you, Kayla. I should be getting back to work. I don't want your dad to think he's wasting his money."

Kayla stepped back reluctantly, wanting to speak with him longer but she knew he was right. There was much work to be done and she had detained the harvest enough already.

"If you should need more water, Mr. Jenkins," Kayla told him. "There is a spigot beside the barn."

He looked at her thankfully.

"You truly are a lifesaver, Miss Roth. You and your father have helped me a great deal already."

Kayla did not know how to respond but Will did not seem to require an answer.

She slipped back into the house and reclaimed her window seat but her book was forgotten. She spent the remainder of the afternoon watching Will working in the field and wondering if *Gotte* had sent him to their farm for a reason.

Kayla waited impatiently for her father to take Hannah to school before hurrying outside to greet Will who was cleaning the stalls. Her father would not be gone long but she wanted to talk to the man again, if only for a short time.

"Good morning, Miss Roth," Will said brightly. She smiled.

"You may call me Kayla," she told him. "I brought you muffins if you are hungry."

She offered them to him and he took them happily. For the third day, he donned the same clothes and Kayla wondered if he had any other garments.

He is obviously not well off. I wonder if that is why Daed brought him here; to help a man down on his luck.

"In that case, you can call me Will," he laughed, taking a bite of the muffin in his hand. His dark eyebrows shot up.

"This is great!" he said. "Did you make this yourself?"

She nodded.

"The Amish can do everything," he sighed. "I knew an Amish girl once. She never failed to amaze me with her talents."

"What happened to her?" Kayla asked curiously, leaning against a stall door. Will smiled thinly.

"She returned to her community. Decided the outside world wasn't for her after all."

Kayla could read the regret in his face but before she could ask anything else, she felt herself grow lightheaded.

Oh no! She thought as bright lights colored her line of sight.

"Kayla?" Will's voice sounded very far away and suddenly she was in his arms as her legs buckled beneath her. She willed herself to take deep breaths and to her relief she did not faint.

"Are you all right?" Will demanded as she regained her footing. Slowly he released her and Kayla stood on shaking legs.

She nodded, shifting her eyes downward.

"I get fainting spells sometimes," she confessed as the spots cleared from her vision. Will's emerald eyes narrowed.

"Have you been to the doctor?" he asked and Kayla bobbed her head.

"I am awaiting test results," she told him, sighing. "They believe it is some sort of blood disorder."

Will's mouth became a tight, white line.

"Is that so?" he asked quietly.

"Kayla! What are you doing in here?" Jeremiah appeared in the doorway, his face pale as he took in the scene before him.

"I – I came to offer Mr. Jenkins some muffins," she murmured, averting her eyes from his shocked face.

"You should not be in here," he told his daughter, shooing her from the barn.

"Thank you for the muffins, Kayla," Will called after her. "I hope you are feeling better."

Jeremiah led the way back to the house and did not say a word until they were inside, whirling to confront Kayla.

"Why were you speaking with Will Jenkins?" he demanded furiously. "I told you that you are to stay in the house."

"Daed, I am growing mad staying in the house!" Kayla protested. "And Will seems a very nice man!"

Jeremiah's expression was indecipherable as he stared at his oldest daughter. He seemed to be considering his next words carefully.

"You are to stay away from Will Jenkins," he told her firmly. "I do not want you anywhere near him, do you understand?"

Kayla's eyebrows knit together.

"No," she answered truthfully. "Of course I do not understand. Why would you ask me to stay away from him?"

"He is not someone whom you should associate yourself," Jeremiah insisted. Kayla stared at him uncomprehendingly.

"*Daed*, if he is such a terrible man, why would you have him come to our home?"

"He not in our home. He is merely helping with harvest. I want you to swear that you will not have any further contact with him. Swear it, Kayla!"

Kayla did not know what to say. She wanted to promise her father that she wouldn't see the Englisher again but she knew her curiosity would not keep her away.

"Kayla!"

She hung her head and nodded, sighing deeply.

"I swear it, *Daed*," she breathed but she wondered if she would be able to honor her oath.

Kayla did not risk going to Will until the next time her father went to the market, three days later. She found herself watching the worker from the window often, willing him to take notice of her and sometimes he would lift his head and acknowledge her with a half-wave but never in Jeremiah's presence.

This makes little sense. Daed brings him from out of town to work and then speaks as if the man is a danger to us.

The previous day, she had gone to the hospital for her test results.

"As we suspected, Kayla, you have a blood disorder called megaloblastic anemia. It can be treated with supplements and dietary changes but it is manageable," the doctor informed her. Kayla nodded, relieved the diagnosis was simple.

"When will I be able to resume my work?" she asked eagerly and the doctor chuckled.

"We will start your injections immediately and you should notice a change within a week or so. The fatigue and dizziness will lessen and you will be back to normal in no time."

Kayla peered at the physician.

"What causes this?" she asked with interest.

"In your case, it is genetic," the doctor replied.

After Hannah left for school and her father for the market, Kayla rushed outside to speak with Will.

"Kayla, you should not be out here," he told her, his jaw locking when she appeared. Kayla was hurt by his words.

"I do not understand; why does my father wish to keep me away from you?" she asked bluntly but Will did not answer as he continued to bale hay.

"I'm sorry," she muttered, turning away. "I only came to tell you that I got my results from the hospital. I have a blood disorder – anemia."

Will's head jerked up to stare at her, his mouth open slightly.

"What kind of anemia?" he demanded. Kayla wracked her mind to recall the proper term.

"Mega...mega..."

"Megaloblastic?"

Kayla smiled.

"Yes, that is it."

Kayla waited for him to return her grin but his face went dark.

"You should go back in the house. You don't want your father to catch you out here."

She stared at him, tears of humiliation filling her eyes.

I thought we had a bond, she thought miserably, chewing on her lower lip.

"Hurry up," Will growled, pointing at the house. Kayla spun, tears spilling down her cheeks as she ran back inside.

Daed was right; I should have just stayed away from him.

"Kayla! *Daed* is yelling!" Hannah cried, flying into the kitchen where Kayla was doing the dishes.

"What?"

"He is yelling at the Englisher!" Hannah insisted, pointing toward the front of the house. Kayla quickly dried her hands on her apron and rushed toward the door. As she pulled open the heavy wood, she heard a car door slam and watched as Will screeched away in his rundown sedan.

Jeremiah stood, his arms folded angrily across his chest as he watched the man leave and Kayla was sure she had never seen him look so intimidating.

"*Daed*! *Daed,* what happened?" she cried, rushing toward him. He whirled to face her, his face undergoing several expressions, settling on near-panic.

"Nothing," he replied gruffly. "Go inside."

"*Daed* please!" she begged. "What happened with Will?"

His eyes narrowed dangerously and he shook his head.

"I made a mistake bringing him here," he muttered, storming toward the house. "Do not mention his name in this house again."

Bewildered, Kayla turned toward the road but of course Will was long gone.

She looked helplessly at her father but she was only staring at his retreating back and Kayla was filled with an inexplicable sense of loss.

He is not coming back, she realized and the thought made her sick to her stomach for reasons she could not comprehend.

Life on the Roth farm returned to normal and as promised, Kayla began to feel better as the treatments took effect.

The harvest went well and Will Jenkins did not return to the district but his memory was fresh in Kayla's mind.

Perhaps one day, Daed will tell me who he was truly and how he came to be here. But she did not have high hopes for that occurring. Jeremiah never brought up the Englisher again and Kayla did not dare.

It was the beginning of November when the letter arrived.

It was slipped between the screen door and it had not been mailed.

Without opening it, Kayla suspected she knew who had written it but as she tore into the envelope, her suspicions were confirmed.

Her hands trembling, she read the letter, her heart thumping wildly.

Dear Kayla, it read. *I have wrestled with whether to write this letter or leave well enough alone as your father wanted. I can't live my life without telling you who I am because I think you deserve the truth. As you know, my name is William Jenkins. Twenty years ago, I met a beautiful girl in Lancaster and we fell madly in love. I mentioned that I once knew an Amish girl and that girl was your mother, Anna. We had plans to marry but one day, I woke up and she was gone. She had left me a letter, much like the one I am writing you, apologizing for her choice and claiming she had made a mistake leaving her community. She begged me not to look for her and I agreed. I left town and moved to Reading, not wanting to run into her. If I had stayed, I would have learned that she married Jeremiah Roth and soon gave birth to a beautiful baby daughter; you.*

If I had not seen your eyes, I may never have known that you were mine but there is no mistaking you are my child.

I did not understand why your father had brought me to your farm until I heard you were sick. Megaloblastic anemia is genetic – I know because I have it also. I suspect Jeremiah was terribly concerned for your health and wanted to learn about your family history. I don't think he ever intended for us to meet and when we did and I learned the truth, he grew angry and banished me from the farm. I want you to know that if I had known you were my child, I would have always been in your life.

You may do what you wish with this information, Kayla. You may choose to never see me again or you may confront your father. Shamefully I do not know you well enough to know how you will react but I would like to get to know you. You are a grown woman and I can't force a relationship on you.

Whatever you do, please remember that your father only did what he did to keep you safe, happy and healthy. If you decide to let him know that you know, go easy on him. He is the only father you have ever had after all.

I have enclosed my phone number and mailing address. I will not hold my breath but I will hold onto hope that you will see me again.

Whatever you choose, know that I support you and love you. I wish you only the best this world has to offer.

Love always,

Will

Tears flowed freely down Kayla's face and the words grew blurry as she read and re-read the letter, her breath escaping in shuddering sobs.

"Oh Gotte, Kayla!" Jeremiah cried, entering the foyer where his oldest daughter stood. "What happened?"

Kayla shook her head and stuffed the letter back into the envelope, wiping her face with the back of her hand.

"Nothing, nothing," she gasped. He stared at her, his face a mask of worry and Kayla had never been filled with so much love for another person.

Does he know I know? Has he been filled with worry for the past nineteen years that the truth would come out and he would lose the daughter he had raised as his own? Kayla could not imagine the pain her father must have endured over the years.

He is the only father I have ever known. He is my Daed no matter what that letter reads.

Impulsively, she threw herself into her father's arm, burying her face in his broad chest.

"I love you, *Daed*," she whispered, inhaling the comforting scent of his dirty work clothes.

"I love you, daughter," he sighed.

In that moment, Kayla knew she would honor her father's wishes and never again bring up Will Jenkin's name in their home.

That did not mean she would never see the Englisher again.

AN AMISH FRIENDSHIP

ERICA FANNING

Living in the Plain community was an absolute joy. In the spring and summer, there were parties and get-togethers in the town square. Young love was in the air and many weddings were conducted. In the fall was the harvest time, where the community would come together as always and help everyone to make sure nothing was left unharvested. Much of what was made and harvested was sold on market days to Englishers passing through from one big city to another. What wasn't sold was saved and stored for the community and for each respective family to help them through the harsh winter. Being in the northeastern part of the country made each winter unpredictable, but they always made their way through it and began to prepare for as many contingencies as possible.

No one could prepare for the contingency of what was about to come upon them.

Rebecca Miller did her usual winter morning duties before the rest of the family was up: feeding the chickens, gathering their eggs, and making sure they were warm. She also checked the garden one last time. It hadn't snowed yet this year, but the ominous clouds above her head and the cold north wind threatened it at any moment. She pulled the shawl she was wearing a little tighter and noticed that there were a few extra vegetables her little brother had missed in his excitement over the stray dog in their yard yesterday. She smiled remembering his little face light up as he ran toward the strange creature. Rebecca's father, Joseph Miller, wouldn't allow the family to get a dog unless they could find one with the right temperament to guard the chickens. Little Matthew was bound and determined that the dog he found was the one.

"I don't think that's how it works, buddy," Rebecca had said. "Besides, this one has a rope around his neck. He probably belongs to someone." Rebecca wasn't going to mention to Matthew that the bullmastiff's massive head gave her some unease. *That thing could eat you alive,* is what she had wanted to say, but instead she went with,

"Let's get you inside. If he's still here when we're done with snack, then we'll talk to Papa about keeping him."

Matthew had been disappointed, but he agreed.

Today, the silence in the air made it seem like not another soul on the earth even existed. Any moment now, it was going to snow. Rebecca hurried inside and no sooner had she walked inside and the snow slowly began falling.

Rebecca loved the snow, it always gave the earth a sort of "do-over" look. She watched it for a few moments before realizing her arms were full of vegetables and eggs. She watched the snow a few seconds more, and then went about her chores for the day.

By mid-afternoon, the snow had been falling steadily now. Matthew was more than excited and wanted to go play with his friends. Papa wouldn't allow it because the Miller's didn't have proper winter attire.

"I don't need you getting sick, my son."

Only three winters ago, Mary Miller, their beloved wife and mother, passed away from pneumonia. Rebecca wasn't above taking her into the nearest town to get medical help, but Papa strictly forbade it.

"No," he had said. "The Miller's haven't been to an English community in over a hundred and fifty years. We're not about to start now. God will heal your Mama."

Both Rebecca and Matthew—who had only been 8 at the time—were scarred toward God and anything taught in church for a long time. Since Matthew was younger, he was able to accept that maybe God allowed it to happen because of some hidden sin that he didn't know about. Rebecca knew better. A loving God wouldn't allow any of His children to be harmed like that. He wouldn't allow a woman who loved Him almost as much as King David in the Bible to be brought down with one of the worst illnesses known to the Plain community. No, she decided she would stay within the community for her little brother, but she wouldn't really serve this supposed God that caused her mother to die.

In fact, most of the time, snow caused her to think very fondly of her mother and how much she loved snow. When it snowed, it was hard for Rebecca to think anything ill toward anyone. She smiled at Matthew trying to convince her to help change Papa's mind.

"Silly boy," she laughed. "You're not going to be able to convince him to let you out. Maybe in the springtime, we'll start making winter clothing so you can go play with your friends next year."

"But that's next year," Matthew pouted. "Maybe James' family has something extra. Please, Rebecca? Can't we at least go ask?"

Rebecca sighed and looked at her father who was standing in the doorway of the living room, where his two children were. He nodded once. She smiled at her little brother. "Let's go."

As soon as Rebecca set a booted foot outside the front door, she knew this snow wasn't going to let up anytime soon. In fact, in the short amount of time it took her and Matthew to get to their neighbors, there was already another quarter of an inch of snow on the ground. As soon as Naphtali Fisher saw the young Miller's out in the snow, she ran outside and covered them both in an extra shawl.

"What do you two think you're doing?" She scolded them as soon as they were inside. "This snow is accumulating so quickly, and Matthew is so little he could get stuck!"

"Mrs. Fisher, I want to play outside with James," Matthew announced as if Naphtali hadn't said anything. "Do you have any extra winter clothes for me?" He looked at her waiting, as she looked at Rebecca in disbelief.

"You came all the way here so he could ask to play out in this?" She looked at Matthew. "No, dear. James is sick. He has the flu. I don't want you to get sick either; maybe you should stay here with us."

"Oh no," Rebecca interjected before Matthew could say anything. "If there's someone sick here, it might be better if we head back. Besides, Papa would be worried for us. Thank you."

Naphtali insisted they take the extra shawls and simply return them when they could. Naphtali was a seamstress by trade and by hobby. Their house was never short of clothing or anything made of fabric.

"You mustn't go by yourselves," Mrs. Fisher insisted one last time. "Luke!" She called for her oldest son and he came around the corner in a flash.

"Yes, Mama?" It had been months since Rebecca had seen Luke Fisher, but she didn't remember him being that handsome. He was well-toned in his body, and he had a lean face with gentle brown eyes underneath a full head of wavy brown hair.

It took Rebecca a moment to realize she had stopped breathing. She knew Mrs. Fisher and Matthew were both talking to her, but she simply remembered walking out the door and it wasn't until they were halfway home that she realized Luke was right there next to her, guiding her steps and making small talk. She knew she was responding, but couldn't remember any of the conversation they had. She did remember him wishing her a goodnight and telling her he would see her in the morning at church.

Church? She didn't realize tomorrow was a church day. "Papa, there's church tomorrow?"

Papa laughed. "I would hope so, my dear. It's Sunday. I know it's not too late, but would you go check on the chickens one last time before it gets too dark?"

Rebecca obeyed, and while she was out there, she tried desperately to remember what she and Luke had talked about on the way home, but all she was coming up with was the way his voice sounded and how steady his hands were whenever she lost her balance. It wasn't until today that she realized having a mate in her life would be an amazing experience, and she hoped that it would be Luke. She was only 16, but she knew she was ready for marriage because that's what the Plain community taught its young women to be prepared for. Rebecca had mastered much of what her mother had taught her in the three years since she had left this earth.

She decided staying outside with the chickens much longer was a bad idea because the wind began to pick up and kick a lot of the snow about. She locked the pen up tightly so the door wouldn't fly open with the wind and quickly returned inside.

"Papa, the weather's starting to get really bad outside. Do you think they'll even had church tomorrow?" Rebecca didn't want to try to travel in this weather if she could avoid it.

"Well, if they ring the bell, then we'll know." The bell was used to assemble the churchgoers, but in extreme cases like this, it was used as a warning to stay where they were. But no sooner had he finished speaking and the church bell rung.

"Quickly! Get as much as you can: food, blankets, clothing. We're going to the church."

The snow was so deep, Matthew kept getting stuck. Papa finally had to carry him to the church. When they arrived, it was already almost full to the brim of people who lived closer than the Miller's.

"How are they going to fit everyone in here?" Rebecca asked absently. Just then Luke Fisher came up to them.

"The basement is open for those who are sick. We still plan on having church in the morning, but we might just move the pews tonight to make room for makeshift beds. Mr. Miller, the men are meeting on the stage to talk about a plan. Would you be willing to help us?"

Papa looked at Rebecca and she nodded. She would stay with Matthew while he helped the men.

"Come, Matthew. Let's get out of the doorway." Rebecca moved them to a warm spot in the sanctuary. There were already a lot of people there, but Rebecca knew they were going to have to get cozy if they wanted to stay alive.

"Excuse me everyone!" It was Luke. Rebecca wasn't sure where the preacher was, but people seemed to listen to Luke just as well. It became quiet except for the people that were still coming in. "Thank you all for coming. Preacher Hostetler has informed me that they are predicting this weather to be some of the worst we've seen in over a hundred years." There were murmurs in the crowd. People were getting nervous.

"There's no need to worry. We have a food stash in the cellar and it looks like some of the other women of the community have brought their own food. We won't ask you to share, but if you want to do so, anything you can give to the community would be greatly appreciated.

"Now, we're still figuring out the logistics of how we're going to bed everyone in here. We want to keep the basement for those who are sick, but we will need volunteers to help care for them. If that's something you want to do, please come stand to the left of the stage."

Rebecca knew in her heart that's what she wanted to do, but she couldn't leave Matthew all alone. She looked at her father, who was standing within visual range, and she caught his eye. He glanced at the growing throng of women, then looked at her and cocked his head. He was okay with her going as long as Matthew stayed put.

"Matthew, I need you to stay here with Miss Mary." The young schoolteacher had been sitting there and had seen the exchange between Rebecca and her father.

"Don't worry about him. He'll be fine," she assured her. Rebecca thanked her and hurried over with the group. As soon as she got over there, Luke announced that they had an ample amount of women and would need others to help cook for the healthy.

"With this many people, it's going to take community effort to make sure we all get out of this alive." Luke continued giving directions for a few more minutes and then dismissed everyone to go to their stations.

Mrs. Stoltzfus was the oldest woman in the group of caretakers, so she quickly took charge and began ordering everyone about as soon as they got to the basement. Since it was late in the evening, they were simply trying to make sure that the sick were comfortable and then began making arrangements for food to be brought down as soon as possible. Rebecca was the youngest of the caretakers, so she did a lot of the running up and down the stairs to make sure the communication stayed open between the floors and the leaders. Basically, she became the messenger girl. She didn't mind so much because that gave her an excuse to see Luke more often and even to talk to him.

By midnight, Rebecca was exhausted and just wanted to sleep. Mrs. Stoltzfus noticed her fatigue and sent her upstairs to sleep with her family. She didn't argue and was glad for the short respite.

When Rebecca woke up the next morning, her throat was on fire and she felt dizzy. She thought nothing of it as she took a swig of some water, washed her face, and hurried downstairs to help. It felt cooler than she remembered and her body shivered. As soon as Mrs. Stoltzfus saw her, she made her sit down.

"Child, you don't look well." The older woman felt Rebecca's forehead. "In fact, you have a fever. Here, we have an extra bed for you right next to James Fisher." Mrs. Stoltzfus led her to the bed and helped her lie down. "I might need your help, but I do believe you're coming down with the flu. It would be best if you stayed still and let the fever pass."

"No, Mrs. Stoltzfus," Rebecca tried to argue. "I'm fine. I think it's just because I didn't sleep well last night. I'll be fine." Mrs. Stoltzfus pushed her down.

"No, child," she insisted. "You stay right there." She helped Rebecca take her shoes off and pulled a blanket up to her chin. "If I see you get up, I will tie you down to this bed."

James Fisher snickered at that. "Oooh, Rebecca's in trouble." He laughed again which led to a coughing fit.

"Now, now," Mrs. Stoltzfus turned from Rebecca to focus on James' coughing. "You must be careful child. Here," she handed him some herbal tea that had been by his bed. "Drink this and your throat will feel better."

"But it's cold."

"I'll go make you some new tea while I cook some up for Miss Miller." She scurried off, making sure to tell some of the other caretakers to keep an eye on Rebecca and James as she went to make more tea.

Rebecca sat up as soon as she was out of sight and kicked the blanket off. "I can't stay here."

"Heh, well don't let Mrs. Stoltzfus find out you're getting up," a voice behind her stated. She spun around to see James' oldest brother Luke standing there, arms folded. "She seemed pretty serious about tying you to the bed."

"You heard that?" Rebecca asked quietly. Luke laughed and nodded as her face flushed. James laughed with his brother.

"Actually, she had to tie me down too, and I've been sick for a week." James seemed very excited about this. "But I know I'm getting better. I already feel like I could run a race!"

Luke went over to his brother's bed and sat on it. "That's great, but you know Mrs. Stoltzfus won't let you go until we can get an actual doctor in here to make sure you're alright."

"Wait," Rebecca stopped him. "We're having an actual doctor come in?" Luke sighed sadly.

"There's almost two feet of snow outside. I don't think anyone's coming for a few days... but last night Mrs. Stoltzfus asked me if I would call a doctor in so that we don't lose people to simple illnesses that the English medical community has found cures for." He lowered his voice before adding, "Like your mother."

Rebecca felt her chest tighten. All those questions of why's and what if's suddenly came back and flooded her thoughts. Suddenly she couldn't catch her breath. Luke had laid her down and was standing over her. He was yelling something, but all she could hear was the quickening sound of her heart, struggling to get oxygen to her brain. The edges of Rebecca's vision began to blur just as Mrs. Stoltzfus came up and sat her up. She was telling her to breathe. She began counting: 1, 2, 3, 4,... The feeling passed as quickly as it came.

"Good job," Mrs. Stoltzfus smiled calmly. "Take a few deep breaths slowly. Do you feel alright now?" Rebecca nodded slowly.

"Rebecca, I am so sorry," Luke said apologetically. "I had no intention of hurting you—"

"Stop." Rebecca didn't want to hear it right now. She just wanted to sleep. She began to lie back, but Mrs. Stoltzfus kept her sitting up.

"You have to drink this first." She handed Rebecca the herbal tea with lemon and honey. Rebecca took a few sips and thanked the woman, who looked at Luke and told him sternly it was time to leave.

Luke looked defeated and helpless, but wasn't about to argue. Slowly, he walked toward the stairs and out of sight.

"Whatever he said to you, honey, don't let it affect you." Mrs. Stoltzfus placed her hand gently on Rebecca's arm. "Sometimes people don't understand what it's like to lose someone they love. He didn't mean anything he said in a harsh way." Rebecca nodded.

"I know," she responded quietly. "It wasn't what he said, but the thoughts that came with it. What happened to me?" The lead caretaker smiled warmly.

"Something we're going to avoid from happening ever again."

As the days went on, some of the younger sick ones began to get better, James and Rebecca among those. As soon as Rebecca was better, she began helping as a caretaker again. She needed something to do to keep her mind off of the fact that they were still stuck in the church. It had been five days and the snow still hadn't let up. Some of the snowbanks were well over ten feet tall and the church doors had been snowed in by day two of the storms. Thankfully the entire community had managed to fit well into the little church place, but many of them were beginning to wonder why they hadn't seen the preacher or his family. Rumors had begun flying that they had gotten stuck in the parish next door. They saw lights on every night from what little could be seen out the windows.

Every night the community got together to pray for the preacher, for the county, for the community's animals that had been left unattended and even for the surrounding English communities. Perhaps they had amenities that the Plain community didn't, but as Luke pointed out during prayer one night, they were still struggling with the same elements and they didn't prepare every year like the community did.

Although Rebecca had been upset by what Luke had said, she also saw how hurt he was by what he had said. She made it a point to go out of her way to talk to him one day during lunch.

"May I sit with you?" She asked politely after she found him sitting alone. He looked up and nodded, his mind seemingly somewhere else. "Are you alright?"

"No," he finally admitted. "The preacher... I know where he is, and it's not next door." Rebecca waited for more, but finally had to ask him to elaborate. "The preacher is the one that went to get a doctor to come look at the sick. I haven't heard from him or anyone, and the cellular phone he provided hasn't had service in three days. I don't want to be depressing, but I don't think he's even alive." He looked up at Rebecca and she saw that he had tears in his eyes. "I'm afraid, Rebecca."

She moved around to his side of the table and held him as he began to cry. The sat like that for a long time before someone called Luke's name. He quickly sat up and wiped his face.

"I have to go."

"I understand." Rebecca was upset that she wasn't able to talk to him, but she knew in her heart that she had forgiven him.

"Thank you," he said as he looked into her eyes, fresh tears welling up. "I feel like I can trust you, and I have always appreciated that about you, Rebecca Miller." He got up and left her sitting there alone.

She knew in her heart that she would never forget this moment... and she would never tell anyone where the preacher really was. She sent up a quick prayer for his safety and hoped he'd made it to town before the storm had gotten too bad, but like Luke she felt in her heart that it was probably too late for him. And that would be the most painful thing for the community to accept.

The next morning, the snow had finally stopped and the sun was shining. It helped to heat the little church some, since there was still so much snow on the windows. The community was abuzz with excitement about how soon they might be able to leave and get back to their abodes to assess the damage. Luke assured everyone that as soon as they could dig their way out of the church and onto the road, people could begin leaving. They were going to have to stay in the church a few more days before that happened though. The men were still putting a plan together on what the next steps were to be.

Indeed, it was another five cold days in the church before the men began to dig a way out of the church. The congregation cheered, and since Rebecca was downstairs helping with the sick, she was sent to see what was happening. The news brought so much hope into the room that many of the sick seemed to get better just by hearing it.

"We need to begin making preparations to leave as soon as possible," Mrs. Stoltzfus told Rebecca and another young girl. "Begin packing everything that we don't absolutely need—any extra bandages, extra tea, that sort of thing. Quickly now!"

"Make way!"

Suddenly there was a hustling coming down the stairs and the three women were almost forced out of the way. There were two men—Luke and Mr. Miller—carrying someone between them... the preacher!

Without any more pleading, Rebecca and the other girl went and retrieved as many extra blankets as they could. The preacher—Troyer—was blue, but he was still breathing. He was wrapped in blankets of his own and had a hat and mittens on, but they didn't know how long he'd been outside.

A crowd had begun forming around the small bed and on the stairs as people were clamoring to see their beloved preacher. Mrs. Stoltzfus shooed them all away with a word and went back to peeling the frozen clothes off of the preacher.

"Set up a curtain for us," she told Rebecca. "We don't need prying eyes to see what our beloved preacher is going through." She ran off to find Naphtali Fisher, the seamstress. She had brought a whole bag of extra blankets and shawls. Maybe she had something to use as curtains.

She found the woman upstairs helping Miss Mary corral the children away from the door in an attempt to keep them warm. There were still men digging their way to the road... Rebecca wasn't sure why the door was still open. She asked them as soon as she reached them.

Naphtali hissed, "I'm not sure, but whoever left it open is about to receive the wrath of God." Rebecca almost forgot why she was there, but as soon as she remembered she spoke in quick sentences. Immediately Naphtali's countenance changed and she went to work finding as much material as she could to help Rebecca make the curtains she needed.

"God bless you child, and God help our preacher." She seemed on the verge of tears; apparently she had been one of the few who hadn't been informed of the new developments. Rebecca nodded and ran down the stairs and began setting up the curtains for more privacy. Mrs. Stoltzfus had the preacher almost completely undressed, and it didn't look good.

She wanted to know how long he had been out there, and where exactly "there" was. Why was he outside by himself? Why didn't he call for help? The questions began forming faster than she could stop them. Her chest began to tighten again and her vision became blurry.

Mrs. Stoltzfus caught it in time and said calmly but firmly, "Breathe, child." Rebecca began counting: *1, 2, 3, 4,...* She took a few deep breaths and hurriedly finished her task.

As soon as she finished, she ran back upstairs to find out why the door was still open. She couldn't find anyone to ask, but the sun on her skin felt nice and warm despite the chill of the winter air. She basked in it only a moment before closing the door firmly and making sure it would still be accessible and easy to open. Luke appeared as soon as she walked away from the door.

"Why did you close the door?" He seemed upset; under the circumstances, that was understandable.

"Because it's cold outside and we don't want the entire community to get sick."

"But we need it open so we can go in and out easily."

"If you need to keep a door open because of convenience, then you shouldn't be living here. There's an English town less than an hour away that will take your convenience. But here, you have to work a little harder to get what you want." Luke pulled back. Rebecca was shocked that even came out of her mouth. "I'm so sorry, I—"

"No," Luke pushed past her, nostrils flaring. "You're not." He slammed the door on his way out, causing those closest to the front of the church to focus their attention on Rebecca. She looked down and walked away as if nothing had happened, but inside she felt as if her world was falling apart. She had no idea how she could possibly have any feelings for Luke Fisher despite all of the things that had happened these past twelve days. She tried to push all of the thoughts out of her mind as she went back downstairs to help Mrs. Stoltzfus and the preacher.

Within a day, a snowplow from the English town had come through and cleared a lot of the snow off of the main road, making the possibility of going home closer than ever. Some people were anxious to what their homes would look like, others were concerned about the animals they'd hastily left behind, but there wasn't one soul who didn't first fear for the future of their preacher and what his fate would be.

A doctor from the English town also came the same day as the snowplow. Luke had managed to get signal on his cellular phone to call the hospital. When the doctor arrived, he immediately called for an ambulance.

"This man has extreme hypothermia. It is literally a miracle that he's still alive. How did this happen?"

Mr. Miller answered, "We found him stuck in a snowbank less than twenty feet outside the door. We don't even know how long he was there. Is he going to make it?"

The doctor shook his head. "I don't know. The damage seems too extensive. I'm not going to make any promises just yet."

Within a few days, they knew the answer. The preacher had passed on. The hypothermia had affected his internal organs too much and nothing they did would fix it.

Luke Fisher was most affected by this, next to the preacher's family. Luke had been mentored by the preacher and was hoping to one day be a preacher in a town of his own one day. Rebecca did what she could to console Luke, but ever since their episode at the church door, Luke had been distant.

With the passing of the preacher and the assessing of their community, everyone's spirits were down. Nearly all the farm animals survived, but the bullmastiff that Matthew had found wandering had died in a snowbank, forever lost to his owners. Matthew cried when Rebecca informed him.

"Why didn't the owners take him back?" There was little consoling the heart of an 11-year-old. Rebecca knew he would bounce back quickly.

There was a lot of damage to houses and to the schoolhouse. Even the church had sustained some damage. Luke took charge and rallied everyone together for one last supper before they officially returned to their homes to rebuild.

Rebecca felt that this would be the best time to try to talk to him before they were simply neighbors again. The way he had treated her for the past week had hurt her every single time she saw him.

"Luke," she began after she came up to the table he was seated at with the preacher's family. She nodded to them and apologized for their loss. "Can we talk in private?"

He didn't seem eager to talk, but he didn't say no. They found a quiet corner and she just let all of her feelings out.

"From the time you walked me home on the first day of snow, to the last argument we had... and everything in between, I've realized something." She stopped and looked away from his face, afraid that she wouldn't be able to finish if she had to look in his eyes for another second.

She continued, "You've been strong, courageous, bold, caring, and passionate. I... I was wondering how you would feel about us courting." She waited a moment before raising her eyes to meet his. She was shocked to see tears streaming down his face, which was soft and tender in that moment.

"Oh Rebecca," he spoke her name as if it was the greatest name in the world. "From the moment your brother became friends with mine, I knew this moment would come. I so desperately wanted you to love me, but was too afraid to do anything because you were going through such a hard time with..." he trailed off, probably afraid Rebecca would have one of her panic attacks. She nodded in understanding.

"Go on."

He moved closer to her, closing the already small gap between them. Her breathing became shallow, but not in the way it had in the past. This was a new feeling. What was this?

"Rebecca Miller," Luke stated, his face only inches from her. "I would love to court you." He kissed her lightly on the lips and a thousand butterflies went off in her stomach at that moment. As quickly as he kissed her, it was over, leaving Rebecca wanting so much more. Luke smiled, seeing the disappointment and confusion on her face.

"You're still only sixteen." He winked. "We'll work up to something better."

"You..." she didn't even know what to say, so she punched him playfully on the arm. He laughed.

"Come on, you should meet the Troyer's."

It was a wonderful thing to see the community come together in their time of mourning and rebuilding. They decided to work on the church and the parish first, since those were the most important buildings in the community. Then they moved onto different barns where the most food was stored. Luke had decided the plan of action would then include working on the houses of the older members of the community, and then those with the youngest children. If the community worked on one thing at the same time, it was accomplished a lot faster. Within two weeks, it was as if nothing had even ravaged the community.

Almost, anyway.

The community was still out a preacher, but the bishop had allowed Luke to preach until they could find a suitable preacher, the Troyer's had to find somewhere else to live, and the community was still mourning the death of their lost shepherd.

Joseph Miller allowed the Troyer's to live with them until a house could be built, so the house suddenly became very full. With Matthew and Rebecca, plus the three young Troyer children, there were five children under the age of 18. Ms. Troyer helped Rebecca with a lot of the cleaning and cooking duties, while Matthew would entertain the children. Mr. Miller was out fixing his barn and tending to his regular winter duties most of the day, so it gave the women some time to talk.

Rebecca could tell that Ms. Troyer was starting to become fond of her father and sometimes she even dropped hints to her Papa that such a thing was happening.

"Papa, you can't shrug this off forever. Mama would want you to be happy and live your life."

"But Rebecca, I am happy. I have my two wonderful children. What else could I need?" Rebecca knew that now was the time to tell him about her and Luke.

"Papa, I won't be here forever." He looked at her, concerned.

"Why?" She laughed.

"Well I'm not dying. Papa, Luke and I are courting! We could be married within the next year! With your permission, of course."

He looked at her for a moment before staring into his hands as if the answer would materialize.

"I don't know what to say," he spoke with a gruff voice. "But I know that I can't try to court someone whose husband has just died."

"But Papa, she's ready when you are." He narrowed his eyes at her.

"How do you know?"

"She talks about you all the time. It's been almost 2 months and she will need help with the children. You're not that much older than her, Papa. At least consider it."

The next night at dinner, there was a special announcement: Ms. Troyer and Mr. Miller were to begin courting, but slowly at first. Papa had decided that they could at least explore the possibility and the best way for that to happen was while they were in the same house together.

"I have a beautiful daughter that will keep me in check for the time being and a son who watches everything I do. I won't let you down." He smiled at Matthew and Rebecca.

The only thing left to do was see if Luke was still serious about courting. Rebecca had left him alone during the rebuilding of the community, but now that they were done and there was a new preacher in place, she knew this was the best time to talk to him.

She found him sitting at an old picnic table on the back side of the church. The weather had warmed up considerably and much of the snow that wasn't directly on the ground had melted. Rebecca joined him and decided to get right to it.

"Are we still going to court?" Luke was quiet for a while and Rebecca began to wonder if he had even heard her. She almost asked the question again until he answered.

"I think so."

"You think so?" He nodded.

"If we do this," they locked eyes, "this is it. I don't go around and 'try out' girls like some of the other guys do. It's either me, or it's the dating game." Rebecca wanted to answer quickly but realized that she needed to think about this. She was only 16 and if this was it, there would be no other. She stared at the table for a few minutes while she thought, but she knew her answer.

"This has always been it." She looked at him. "At the end of the day, it's always you and me, leading the way. We make sure our families are provided for and that everyone is safe. Why not do it together?"

"Wow," Luke said after a minute. "That was really poetic. Do you always talk like that?" Rebecca shrugged.

"I guess you bring the poet out in me."

"Either that, or I bring out a panic attack."

They laughed as Luke bent down and threw some snow in Rebecca's direction. This was truly the man she wanted to be with, and she knew that nothing else would be so important as this decision here and now. This beautiful friendship would turn into a beautiful romance... and that was the best thing for Rebecca and for her father. She was glad for this new stage in life and wanted nothing else than to enjoy this snowball fight with the man that would soon become her husband.

THEIR AMISH LOVE

ALICE EVANS

<u>Prologue:</u>

The tears begin to pool at Laura's feet as she rests her head in her hands. Propped up against the window frame, she begged for the pain to stop as she watched the world around her turn. They couldn't see. They wouldn't care enough to try. As the day drug on, one more piece of her shattered existence faded away as their smiles and laughter filled the outreaches of her mind. As their days rolled on, all of the things she had so desperately pushed down into the back of her mind had begun to rip her soul to shreds. Nothing in her life had ever been easy, but she never once complained; that wasn't who she was. Laura Miller stood in the face of adversity and simply stated that God had a plan for her and if this adversary is what He intended for her, she was willing to stand her ground with Him by her side.

For the first time in thirty-five years of living, however, she couldn't. For the first time, she couldn't hold onto the singular force in her life. Because if she aligns herself with Him, then she must also agree to the terms that the same person who is on her side is the same person on... *his.* After giving him ten years... ten years of devotion, love, and care, she must remain silent. Her cries muffled, her pain ignored. Then all at once, the pain becomes too much and as she clutches her chest, Laura falls to her knees; knocking into the bookcase.

As the Good Book falls beside her, her vision clears just long enough to read one verse; Isaiah 64:8. *"Yet you, LORD, are our father. We are the clay, you are the potter; we are all the work of your hand."* Whether fate, need, or celestial intervention, Laura dries her face and uses the limits of her strength to rise to her feet. She knows that whatever she chooses to do next, it will change everything. There is nothing she can do, but she can no longer sit around in passive silence. She must confront her fear and remain unshaken in her faith... but as she turns, her mind flings back once more to before this all began.

"how did I end up here..."

<u>Chapter One</u>

You are one in a million; there never has been or will there ever be someone who is exactly like you. Laura Miller heard this phrase uttered by every mother after she helped them to deliver their child. Hearing those few words always sparked a great warmth that would wash over her and spread throughout the home being created. This thought, of course, was always followed by a murmured chuckle as Laura realized how juvenile she was being. Despite these thoughts entering her mind, she had decided many years previous that she could not be happy without her job as a midwife. From the newborn coos to the mother's tears the moment she gets to hold her child for the first time, Laura found that nothing else in this Earth bound life could ever bring her the same joy.

For this, she considered herself very lucky. Some people are not as fortunate as she was in finding that her work and her passion in life were aligned completely. Whether due to financial constraints, personal inability, or and other number of factors, not everyone is afforded the same luxuries she praised God for everyday. As she packed up her kit to go into town, the hired hand her husband had hired to help fix the roof knocked on the door jam before entering.

"Ms. Miller, there's someone here to see you, ma'am."

"Thank you, Jeremiah, you can send them in." Jeremiah nodded his head and moved aside for a woman to enter her home.

"Thank you, ma'am for welcoming me into your home. I am sure you are quite busy so I won't take up much of your time-"

"Slow down, child. My schedule should not concern you. Besides, unless the Lord has any plans for Susan Price's child to be born two months early, my schedule is all but cleared for the day." The small woman stood in front of her, and though she smiled, her body language betrayed her true feelings. Short in stature, and thin in frame, if her cheeks hadn't been so flushed, Laura would have been convinced that she was sickly or malnourished. Scanning over the woman's stance and overall demeanor, Laura could tell that something wasn't quite right with the picture she was seeing.

"Would you care to sit?" Laura floated her hand to usher the woman into her kitchen. It took the woman a minute to collect herself as she situated herself in Laura's grandfather's handmade chairs. "What's your name, dear?"

"Sarah. Sarah Fisher."

"Oh, you are Ihrm and Mary Fisher's daughter right?" Sarah nodded her head briskly. "I don't think I've ever had the pleasure of meeting you. Though, somehow I feel like you already know me."

"Please don't think me intrusive. Susan is a friend of mine and she told me that you were the best person in town to speak to about... well really anything." At this point, Sarah's words flew from her lips. As if she had been bottling up her words for far too long.

"Susan speaks too highly of me. Maybe you would be better speaking to Preacher King. He lives just up the road if you would like me to escort-"

"NO!" The strength and anguish in her voice startled Laura; and frankly would have sent her reeling if she had been standing. Noticing the confusion her exaltation had invoked, Sarah quickly searched to find the words to save face. "What... What I mean to say is.... Well..."

"You want to talk to a woman, not a man is what I am gathering. Is that right?" Sarah nods her head vigorously.

"It's not that I feel shameful or like I am doing something wrong that the preacher can help me with.... I feel I just needed to talk to someone like you; especially after hearing about how helpful you have been for Susan throughout her pregnancy." Laura watched as Sarah's hand left her lap and began cradling her stomach. Though it had gone unnoticed before, Laura could now see a distinguishable outline.

"Sarah, are you pregnant?"

"Yes. Or at least, I think I am. My husband says we are so lucky to be blessed so soon after our wedding, and I agree..."

"But?"

"But... I wish I had been given more time to prepare for this. What if I mess something up and end up hurting my child?"

"The fact that that is your biggest concern proves to me that you will do nothing of the sort. Believe me, I have sat with many an expectant mother and they all share the same fears brewing in your mind. You fear that the love you have won't be enough; you worry that your husband won't care for you the same after the baby comes; you fear that you will somehow mislead the child and that he won't follow in our ways; I have heard every fear and worry in the book."

"And what do you tell them?"

"I tell them that it is all going to be alright. The Lord does not give His people something that they cannot handle; but that doesn't mean that it is sinful or shameful to ask for help. We all have good and bad days, but being honest about that makes it easier to make it to the other side." Sarah's face began to brighten as Laura's words of encouragement and love began to sink in.

"Thank you, Miss."

"You may call me Laura if you like." Sarah's smile then widened to encapture her whole face and the color had begun to return to her skin.

"Thank you Laura."

<u>Chapter Two</u>

"That's Mrs. Miller to you, girl." A gruff voice filled the house as Laura gripped the cloth in her skirt.

"Ephraim, please."

"I'd keep my mouth shut if I were you, Laura." Laura pushed her energy into her feet to stand, but she couldn't make herself move.

"I'm not sure who you are and I will apologize if I frightened you. However, I need to speak with my *wife* and I am going to ask you only once to leave my house." Sarah's eyes darted between the scene unfolding before her eyes. She nodded her head once before quickly exiting. Laura wished to have the courage to express herself before

Sarah's shadow escaped the stoop, but her eyes blazed with fear as her husband walked over to her.

A statuesque man, Laura always considered herself to be quick lucky to "land him." Before her father died, he insisted that he see Laura be married to a God-fearing, stand-up man who could take care of her. From the moment they were introduced, Laura was inexplicably smitten. From his dark auburn hair to his piercing green eyes with the little blue flecks, not only was he a man of God, but he was the kind of man she always imagined herself with. Less than three months after their courtship began they were married. The wedding was a large affair, larger than any other the town had experienced and they were gilded with praise and admiration for being the most successful match the community had ever seen.

But what happened behind closed doors was different. The first few months, even years were fine. They were happy and nothing seemed remiss. But as they approached their fifth wedding anniversary, something in him changed. As much love and support that Laura would afford her husband, he stopped smiling. The person the town saw during the day was not the man she would come home to at night. The man she knew and believed to be kind, open and charitable turned mean-spirited, harsh and oftentimes rude. Laura, despite all of this, gave him the benefit of the doubt. Maybe the business isn't doing well, maybe he isn't feeling good; perhaps he's just having a bad day... all these things and more ran through her head as she created excuse after excuse for his differing behavior towards her and others. This continued for another five years and unbeknownst to her, their tenth anniversary was about to pass them by.

Laura's inner monologue of running through the changes in her husband's behavior became readily apparent to him as he threw his hat down.

"What are you thinking about? What?"

"Ephriam, are you alright?"

"What, you work as a midwife and you fancy yourself a doctor?"

"That's not what I meant," Laura's mood began to fall as her husband's harsh expression fell on her heart. "I'm just worried about you. I am your wife, you should be able to confide in me about everything, and if something is going on that I need to know about-"

"Why would I talk about anything of any importance with you when you are never around?"

"I don't understand..."

"What, you have time for every terrified girl bringing new life into this world, but you can't afford me anytime at all?"

"When have I ever prioritized my work over my love for you?"

"When haven't you?"

"Ephraim, please, you aren't making any sense. What do you want from me?"

"Why? Am I scaring you?" Laura, now stood across the room, had laced her fingers around the locket encircling her neck. Her eyes unable to flutter from his. As piercing and afraid his expression made her, she could never seem to remove her gaze. As much and as often he confused her and conjured up fear in her heart, her love for him was unyielding.

"What, you can't find the words?"

"I don't know what you want me to say. I have sat beside you day after day as you changed before my eyes. My love for you has never faltered and even now with these accusations all I ask is that you are honest with me about what you want. Something has been bothering you for so long, but you won't talk to me." Laura could feel her own voice increasing in intensity. "Just tell me what you want! I can't read your mind!" Angry tears flow down her cheeks as she can no longer hide how unhappy she had become.

Ephraim felt every tear as if it were his own as they rained down his wife's cheeks. He knew what he was doing hurt her, but something in him was telling him that it was for the best. The hurt she felt now is what she deserved for taking him for granted all of these years.

"You want to know what I want?" Laura's eyes close as more tears stream down her face and shakes her head; as if begging him to reveal his pain to her. As he stares at her, looking for any shred of sincerity, he states his desires through the use of one word.

"Quit." And with that, Laura's heart broke.

<u>Chapter Three</u>

They didn't speak the rest of the night. Laura's heart hung heavy in her chest as she laid herself to bed that night. She didn't realize how unhappy her work had made him. But as these thoughts plague her mind, she feels Ephraim lay down beside her. Every bone in her body wants to roll over and wrap her arms around him; to provide him some sort of comfort that he can't seem to find within himself. As she shifts her weight in the bed, she feels him turn away from her, as if knowing the desires in her heart. Muffling her tears, she closed her eyes and drifted off.

Laura often found solace in her dreams, believing that God would often speak to her through her dreams and help to guide her towards finding the answers she needed. She prayed before finally drifting off to sleep for Him to give her a sign or to help her understand her husband's sudden fury with her desire to continue working. Tonight, however, it was not an abstract, objective vision but a walk through her own memories. She flies through her inner timeline until everything stops and she lands in a memory from so many years ago she had nearly forgotten about it's passing...

"Are you enjoying yourself, Laura?" Laura watches on as her younger self walked through the meadow with the younger version of the man she loved inquired of her feelings.

"This is lovely Ephraim. How did you manage to find this place?"

"Well while everyone else went out on Rumspringa I stayed behind to help my father and mother in their shop. They are going to hand it over to

me one day, you know and I thought then was as good a time as any to get started learning the business."

"I'm sure they greatly appreciated that. But didn't you ever regret not getting to go out and experience the world before beginning your life?" Laura, watching on, did not take that much stock into his responses or expressions that day, but she now finds herself unable to look anywhere else. She hid behind the seemingly singular tree in the vast valley she found herself remembering; though she chastised herself for hiding because as this is just a memory why should she be hidden? She, after all, was the one who needed to figure out why God was showing this to her.

"Why would I leave when I have everything I could possibly need right here? Besides, now that you are back, why would I ever need to leave?" Both Laura's blush uncontrollably.

"Ephraim, please."

"What? Do you know how distressed I was when you left?"

"We had never met before our fathers introduced a few months ago."

"No, but I saw you when you left town that day."

"You did?"

"As I saw you with your suitcase in tow begin to walk away from town, I ran up to the roof of my parent's shop to get a better look at you. From the instant I laid eyes on you I thought you were the most beautiful girl I had ever seen."

"Ephraim-"

"I didn't know how long you were going to be gone, but I knew that I would wait as long as it took for you to return."

"But you didn't know me. I could have been deranged or incompatible... what made you do a silly thing like that?" Ephraim stopped in his tracks, turning back to face her. Plucking a bright yellow field from her feet, he places it behind her ear; caressing her face as his hand falls to lock with hers.

"Something in me just knew. Whether that was God or my heart, I believe that He wanted me to know to wait for you to return. I mean I didn't think it would take four years, but better late than never I guess." Laura lightly wacks Ephraim with her free hand as he pulls her with him, running through the meadow.

Laura awoke as she felt herself intertwine with her past self as she was pulled into the meadow by the man snoring loudly beside her. Rubbing the vision from her eyes, the room was pitch black. She had no new answers, just further confusion.

"Why that memory?" She pondered aloud.

"Go back to sleep, Laura."

"Ephraim! I'm sorry, did I wake you?"

"Just because I'm angry doesn't mean I am not still concerned when my wife wakes up in the middle of the night for no discernable reason." Laura feels a smile and a small spark light in her chest. "Go to sleep, Laura."

She reaches to place a hand on her husband's shoulder, but finds herself holding herself back. She found herself at a disadvantage to her husband. Though she had never questioned his love for her, she never knew the depth of his love for her. That memory from so long ago that was tossed aside because of a frivolous girl's temperament now broke this woman's heart. A man who loved her so much to wait for her to return to their world couldn't answer for why she stayed away for so long. As much as she wanted to, everything they had built together would be destroyed if she did. Letting loose a sigh, her head falls back towards her pillow and she closes her eyes trying to escape the guilt boiling in her gut.

<u>Chapter Four</u>

When she woke up in the morning, Ephraim was nowhere to be found. She ventured around the house and both the front and the back yard before re-entering the kitchen. As she runs her fingers absentmindedly over the splits in the wooden table, she yelped as her fingers brush a piece of paper, slicing her fingers. As she tended to her fingers, she looked down to find a crumpled piece of paper lying on the table. Laura felt a stone lodge in her heart as she flattened out the piece of paper to read its inscription:

Laura,

I will be home tonight at five, at which point we need to discuss your leaving your work to come stay at home and take care of things around the house. Please be home on the time I have spoken or else we will be discussing other matters with Preacher King.

Yours.

It was hard for Laura not to crack a smile at the way he signed the note. As heartwrenching a message, his signature took her back to before they were married and he signed all his letters - not with his name or a funny anecdote, but with one small little word to prove to her that he was hers utterly. Because of his signature still finding its way onto this note, she clings to the hope that they will overcome the situation they are facing together. However... that also means she will have to tell her husband the truth.

At this exact moment of pivotal decision making, Laura is startled by a knock on the door, followed by a loving voice.

"Laura? It's Susan. I've brought Sarah with me, are you home?" Laura crossed the room to the door.

"Hello Susan, Sarah. Would you like to come in?" As the women enter into Laura's home, it is clear they notice something is off about Laura.

"Are you sure? I mean, we can come back once you've changed and fixed yourself..." Laura immediately takes her hand to her head and feels the tousled mess her hair had become. Embarrassed, she asked the woman to wait in the kitchen while she quickly through on a new outfit and wrangled her hair into a bun tucked neatly at the nape of her neck.

When she reemerged, the woman seem relieved that she has returned to her normal state.

"What brought you to my doorstep this morning? Is it labor pains? I promise it's probably just a false alarm. I've yet to be wrong about false labor."

"No, no, nothing like that. Sarah came to see me yesterday after leaving here yesterday and I wanted to come and check in to make sure that everything is alright because clearly something is going on and to be honest we are worried." Words fell from Susan's lips, quicker and more abrasive than she meant them.

"What Susan means is, are you and Ephraim okay? It just seemed so out of character for the behavior I saw yesterday..."

"We just want to know that you are okay and we want you to know that you can talk to either of us whenever you need to about anything. You have done so much for the women of this town that it seems only right that we pay it forward in their stead." Laura felt both a wave of acceptance and terror at their words of encouragement. After fifteen years of keeping her secret, could anyone forgive her? Her breaths catch in her throat as she attempts to decide whether or not she will allow them in or continue hiding her grief from more people who care about her. As she took one long inhale and exhale, she lets her gaze linger between the two women.

"What I say here does not leave here." The women sit to the front of their chairs, leaning in to see what could possibly have the strong woman they know and love so scared. "Susan, you knew me before I went away."

"We were in school together and you introduced me to my husband. I'm forever grateful you brought him into my life."

"Well, yes. But after I came back from my Rumspringa, you were the first person I went to see." Laura paused to gather thoughts. "You didn't question why I had been gone so long, you didn't tell me how much you missed me, and you didn't ask fifty questions all at once;

because the one question you did ask was enough." Susan gathered her memories in her mind to find what Laura was referring to.

"I... I asked you what happened because you looked awful. We thought that the family you had stayed with had hurt you in some way. I never really believed you when you said that they were nothing but kind to you. How could they have been when you came back looking like that?"

"What did you look like?" A perfectly innocuous question, fell on the harsh expression of Susan; letting Sarah know that it may not have been the place for that line of questioning.

"It's alright Sarah; Susan, you remember better than I do surely." Susan, annoyed at Laura's demand for her to recount a time in her life she would rather forget.

"She looked half-dead. From the bruising around her eyes, the pale white her hair had turned, the sheer loss of body weight... we were convinced you had been tortured or worse."

"In a way, I was... but not in the way you are thinking."

<u>Chapter Five</u>

Sarah and Susan stare intently at their confidant as she searches for the right way to express herself.

"Okay... so I am going to walk you through what happened to me, and I need you to just sit and listen. Please no interjections or I am not sure I will be able to make it through this." The women nod their heads in solidarity. Laura shuts her eyes and enters into her past.

It was the third month I was in New York City. The family I was staying with took me to Times Square, this big plaza full of tourists and so many different kinds of people. It was beautiful. We went and saw a Broadway show and on our way home, I began to feel a bit off. I had been getting tired a lot recently and the pain in my stomach wasn't new either. Though I all but actually drug my heels into the ground, they took me to the hospital. After doing some tests, a tall, brooding man in a white coat came to the side of my bed. He looked stern - but that is how everyone in that world looked. I will never forget what he told me.

"Miss. I'm not quite sure how to tell you this, but you have end stage ovarian cancer." Though I didn't know what his words meant, I knew that it was something incredibly serious.

"Basically, the cancerous cells have formed cysts on your ovaries causing you the abdominal pain and the feeling of exhaustion from your body trying to fight the diseased cells. It is rare for someone of your age to have this aggressive of a strain unless you were predisposed to this condition genetically. Now, this is going to sound indelicate, however, did either your mother or grandmother have any issues like this?"

"Did they?"

"Sarah! What did she say about interruptions?" Laura let out a wry laugh as they squabbled. When they looked up at her, Susan gestured for her to continue.

"My mother died when I was born, and I never met my grandmother." The doctor proceeded to look at my chart, wringing his head.

"We need to get you booked into an ER immediately to do an emergency hysterectomy. You won't live more than six months without the operation."

"Don't worry Laura, we are taking care of everything. We will take care of any expense to make sure you can go back home healthier than you left."

"Wait... wait... what is a hysterectomy?"

"Well... again, I am sorry about how this sounds, but we need to go in and remove your ovarian tract because - if you want to look at your scans - there is no hope for saving them and the cancer is already beginning to spread. Unfortunately, as this procedure is highly invasive, you will have to undergo serious treatment and the recovery period could be anywhere from six months to two years." Laura's heart fell to her feet. She couldn't believe what she was being told.

"Okay. Well what are the long term effects of this procedure? Like, if I get it I can live a normal, healthy life?"

"Completely. The only thing that will be adversely affected will be that you will not be able to conceive naturally."

"Wait a minute... you - you can't have children?" Susan's frame has shifted from the front of her chair to the back; as if all the wind had been knocked out of her.

"I fought getting the procedure... but I wasn't getting any better. And the thought of my father being here all alone, I knew I had to get better to come home to him."

"Oh my word."

"The procedure took a lot out of me, and I had to be put into this coma thing so that my body could begin to heal itself. I woke up almost eight months later; healed, but heartbroken."

"Why have you kept this from everyone? I mean, you almost died... Wait," Sarah's brain catches up with her words, "does Ephraim know?"

"No... but I feel I am going to have to tell him soon. He wants me to quit being a midwife."

"What! NO! I need you and Sarah is going to need you as her pregnancy progresses. You are the best midwife in the whole county."

"Susan, did you ever wonder why I wanted to be a midwife?"

"I just assumed that people in your family had or you just liked helping people."

"Though I do enjoy helping people on one of the most pivotal and important moments in their lives, there is a far more selfish reason I work so hard and so long with all of you. It's because when I help women deliver their babies, I am able to - just for a split second - experience the same euphoria they do and I feel less broken."

"But you aren't broken, Laura..." Sarah reaches out a hand to comfort her friend but Laura bats it away as her hot, angry tears boil over onto her cheeks.

"How would you know? Both of you have children growing in your stomachs and- and I can't have children."

"The Lord must've had a larger plan for this. I mean, you may not be able to have children, but ask any woman you have helped and they will tell you that if you hadn't been there they wouldn't be sure that they would have been able to make it through in one piece." Sarah and Susan began to cry with Laura.

"I-I just don't know how I am going to be able to tell Ephraim. I know I have to, that has become clear."

"How do you think he will react?" Susan inquires as she places her hands on Laura's.

"Why don't you turn around and ask him yourself?"

<u>Chapter Six</u>

Ephraim's gruff voice catches in his throat. Laura's eyes go wide, unable to look behind her to where his voice came from. Sarah and Susan look up to meet Ephraim's gaze, before they look back down at the terrified Laura.

"We are going to leave you two to talk." Susan stands up and grabs Sarah's wrist to guide her to the door. Sarah stalls for a second to hug Laura and only released as she whispered in her ear,

"Take a deep breath and just tell him. It will be okay." Sarah smiles as she is drug away by Susan, leaving Ephraim slouched against the door frame as Laura shrunk back into her seat. Nothing was said and no one moved for what felt like eons. Finally, because otherwise she felt she was going to go mad, Laura raised her tear stained face to ask,

"How much did you hear?"

"Every word."

"I thought you weren't going to be back until tonight."

"I... I left... well now I can't remember what I left, are we really not going to address what I just heard?"

"Look, we were fine before when you didn't know and we can be fine again. Just pretend you don't know anything and then I can go back to compartmentalizing the guilt I feel and you can go back to being angry with me or whatever you want. Just please... please pretend this didn't happen this way."

"Would you ever have told me if I didn't find out this way?" The silence between them was deafening as Laura decides that she can no longer go on lying.

"No. I wasn't. After this long, too much time had passed. And after your behavior shift a few years ago I couldn't risk you using this knowledge about me as ammunition against me to nullify our union. Because for whatever reason you are mad at me, there has not been on second, one moment since we met that I have not been completely and wholeheartedly in love with you."

"I am such a fool." Laura's sobs catch in her throat as she feels her husband approach her back and squat down in front of her to meet her gaze. "All this time I thought you were working as a midwife because you didn't want your own kids, while the whole time you have been keeping this secret from me because you were scared I would leave you? How poor a husband am I that I led you to believe that you couldn't rely on me absolutely in every aspect of your life?" Laura broke down into heart wrenching, gut punching sobs as she throws her arms around her husband. His hands pushing her closer to him, holding her tighter than he ever had before.

"I - I just couldn't live with the thought of you hating me for deceiving you for all of these years. It wasn't that I didn't want to stay home and be a housewife, it was that I couldn't stay home and be a housewife because I lack the ability to do the one thing housewives are supposed to give their husbands: children..." Laura stopped a moment to breathe, "I... I can't give you children."

"Why didn't you just talk to me about this?"

"Because I am ashamed. If not only for the fact that I accepted outside medical care, I became ashamed of my secret and it felt as if too much time had passed and I had missed my opportunity." Ephraim pulls back for a moment, taking his hand and wiping away her tears.

"I never want to hear you tell me that you are ashamed of yourself ever again. If anyone should be ashamed it is me. I didn't trust in your love for me and I didn't discuss my issues with our circumstances openly with you. I went and stewed behind your back only causing more anxiety for you and breaking our relationship even further."

"But my lies are what started it all. I am so sorry Ephraim, can you ever forgive me?"

"Laura, you are the woman I love, have always loved, and will always love. As angry and bitter as I had become, this was the last possible thing I could have conjured up to have been the reason for your neglectance to want to stay in the home."

"I love you too." Laura's sheepish confession caused Ephraim to cradle her chin in his hands, trying to find his eyes in hers. When she did finally meet his gaze, she saw something so wonderful, she thought she would never stop crying: Ephraim was smiling.

<u>Epilogue</u>

It would take much time and counseling from the elders of the community, but soon after all was revealed, Laura and Ephraim were on the path to rebuild their life together. As strong as their relationship had been, without their revelations, Laura had been sure that they would have never lasted. It has been three years since Laura was able to tell her husband the truth; and in those three years, Laura and Ephraim's relationship became strong. To show his solidarity with her work, he built her an addition on their house. In which she counseled and provided assistance to young - and oftentimes frightened - mothers-to-be; she also used the space to teach other women the skills she had acquired so she could give him the gift he wanted: more time together.

Relationships have their ebbs and flows, but trust is the stone that can either break the walls or build the castle. After their trust in eachother had been utterly destroyed by misunderstanding, it took a long time to build each other back up; and they may never finish rebuilding... But by growing together, they found that they could do anything, just so long as they had the Lord in their hearts and each other in their eyes. For God gives us nothing that we can't handle, and if it becomes too hard, He gives us each other to find solace in.